SCANDAL POINT

SCANDAL POINT

Manju Jaidka

RUPA
PUBLICATIONS INDIA

Published in 2011 by
Rupa Publications India Pvt. Ltd.
7/16, Ansari Road, Daryaganj,
New Delhi 110 002

Sales Centres:

Allahabad Bengaluru Chennai
Hyderabad Jaipur Kathmandu
Kolkata Mumbai

This is a work of fiction.
Some of the names of characters and places are
taken from history but they are incorporated into the novel
only for the purpose of telling a story creatively.
There is no intention to defame any individual or institution.

Printed in India by
Rekha Printers Pvt Ltd.
A-102/1, Okhla Industrial Area, Phase-II,
New Delhi-110 020

With love and affection
to the generous spirit of the
Late Maharaja Rajinder Singh
and to the
Late Sardar Kartar Singh Ahluwalia
(Papaji, whom I never met)

And also to
all their survivors, scattered across the face of the earth

CONTENTS

CONTENTS

ACKNOWLEDGEMENTS

I am indebted to a number of people for assorted fragments of a forgotten story which I have tried to piece together in *Scandal Point*. A chance remark here, a comment there, a piece of historical information handed down the generations, the undying romance of Shimla, the fading grandeur of Patiala, reminiscences of a lost generation and the moral support of friends and family, all interwoven with the imagination, form the warp and woof of my novel. How do I possibly acknowledge all these sources of inspiration, some real and concrete, others abstract and intangible? I cannot thank them enough.

Chitra Paul (my sister) and Manpreet Kang (of IPU, Delhi) deserve a special mention for going through my manuscript with a fine comb and reassuring me of its worth; my daughters, Bulbul and Kokil, for having faith in me; my husband Vickram, son Raju, and son-in-law Rahul for their silent, unobtrusive support. Thank you, my lovelies!

PROLOGUE

SIMLA, 1952

Scandal Point. This is where my story begins. This place where four roads meet.

I am no Oedipus but my life seems to have followed the same pattern. In Oedipus's story there were three roads that met at a fatal point, determining his destiny. One led from the temple of Apollo, another from Corinth and a third took him straight to Thebes – to his doom. Fleeing from his destiny, Oedipus headed straight into the inexorable clutches of his fate.

From this spot where I stand, one road leads upwards to the ridge, curving towards the church. A lower road, like a fork, runs down to the Mall Road in the same direction, touching the Town Hall, the police station, and Gaiety Theatre on its left. Gaiety stands in the wedge between these two roads, the upper and the lower, with its main entrance on the Mall and an exit from the upper ridge.

The third road leads in the opposite direction towards the general post office and the Kalibari Mandir. A little lower, the Mall continues in the same direction towards the Rashtrapati Niwas that was once the Viceregal Lodge.

I stand here at this juncture where these four roads come together. Actually it is just two roads that converge to touch at this point and diverge again, so it seems as though there are four roads instead of two. To the left of me is a police post marking the centre of the crossroad. This is Scandal Point. On my right is the statue of Lala Lajpat Rai, the freedom fighter, erected in 1948, a year after Independence.

Independence? Freedom? They say this country is free. And yet what does freedom mean to me? What could freedom mean to one who is imprisoned in the tangles of a chaotic history?

In a network of memories, in dark musty labyrinths of what might have been, what must have been, and what could possibly have been?

I probe the recesses of my mind. I delve into the remote corners of the past. Into dimly recollected remembrances, scenes and events; vague snatches of conversations heard as a child. I am no Oedipus but my life seems dictated by a similar inexorable fate, surrounded by enigmas. I know the answers, yet at the same time, I know them not. I do not know the facts. I do not know what truth is and what illusion. All these years I have been trying to piece together scraps of information from random quarters to help me decipher the destiny that was writ for me. Trying to complete a half-told story that eludes completion. I still seek answers to a thousand questions. Questions I was forbidden to ask all these years. Questions that fell on deaf ears whenever I dared to utter them. I have finally come here to face reality. To reconstruct my history. Piece by piece, one jagged clue at a time. I must know where these four roads lead, where the story ends.

I must complete the picture, even if it destroys me.

ATTAR SINGH

Let me go back to the beginning in Lahore. The year is 1900.

I spent most of my time together with my two brothers and a sister in the precincts of the kothi. We were pampered and also often chided from time to time. We called our parents bibi and baba: they were strict but like all parents loved us and wanted the best for us. We were sent to the same school and then to the same college – Aitchison College in Lahore, the best in the region. Being a member of its managing committee, baba had clout there. We were all given special treatment.

My brothers were already in high school when I was yet to be admitted in kindergarten. The age difference was considerable. As for behen-ji, my sister, when I was young she was old enough to carry me around on her hip. She told me stories at night when bibi was busy attending on baba. I was the baby of the family and everyone pampered me. Sometimes they called me prince or raja.

I have hazy memories of bibi's brother, Rajen mamu who would often visit us from Patiala. He sometimes came entourage, accompanied by his courtiers and servants. We loved the grandeur of his dress, the bright pink turban he sported on his head, the many pearl necklaces he wore around his neck, the shining beaded belt around his waist, the sparkling stone with the feather in his turban – everything about him was dazzling. Once he drove up in his motor car and we all piled into the vehicle and went berserk as he drove us around the old city of Lahore, the Anarkali market and the Shalimar Bagh. Mamu would bring lots of gifts for us. I recall that it was my sixth birthday when he had got special gifts for me – a new set of clothes, shimmering gold stuff with matching *juttis* from Patiala. That was the last time I saw him. He promised to give me a motor car when I came of age, also promising me a trip to Patiala where I would be allowed to stay with him in his palace.

But that was not to be.

It was in the middle of a cold and wintry night just after Diwali when bibi came into my room. I was fast asleep and she sat by my pillow stroking my hair. I was half aware of her presence until a sob shook her body and a tear dropped on my face. Mamu, she said, had died in a hunting accident.

I did not know what to say. I knew that meant no more gifts from Patiala. It meant no motor car when I came of age. But did it mean something more? Bibi was babbling: 'My poor unfortunate baby, my little darling.' She held me tight.

My brothers were in the same room and continued to sleep through the night. Bibi did not hold them close, nor did she weep over them. She did not call them the poor unfortunate baby or darling.

After the untoward visitation from bibi lamenting over mamu's death, she did not mention mamu again. Life continued as before – school, play, sports and some religiosity too. Behen-ji, my sister, rarely joined us in our games. She seemed to have grown up suddenly and before I realised, she had turned into a young woman. Bibi and baba gave her away in marriage to Sardar Balkar Singh, a tall young man with a sharp nose, owning agricultural lands around Amritsar. Then it was just my brothers and I. They went to college and I went to school. They, veer-ji and bhai-ji, went to England for further studies in law. I told bibi and baba that I too would like to go to England when I grew up but bibi told me I could never go to *vilayat*.

Why? I asked bibi. Why could I not go to England like my brothers? But she remained tight-lipped and avoided an answer, telling me that she needed at least one son by her side. This was the first unanswered question that now comes back to haunt me.

I yielded then and did not broach the subject again.

In the winter of 1912, soon after Diwali, when I was nineteen, bibi was taken seriously ill. She wanted me by her side all the time. Baba, worried, spared no effort in getting doctors and medicines. He would come home early and sit by her side, holding her hand, talking to her softly. When he was not around I would attend on bibi.

Our efforts came to naught. Bibi deteriorated all the more and became so weak that she could not get up from bed. Her face was wan and her eyes had a wasted look. But when I sat beside her she would hold my hand gently and smile.

One day she told me that she was about to die.

'Don't be silly, bibi,' I said to her. 'You need to sleep. You are tired.'

'No, *puttar*. I know my hour has come and I have to go now,' she repeated.

Her body was hot; endless thoughts perturbed her. I pressed her hand reassuringly and said: 'I will not let you go, bibi.'

She did not smile. 'No *puttar*, look, they have come for me.' Her eyes were wide and clear.

'Who has come for you?' I stood puzzled.

'Can't you see? They are standing at the door, waiting to take me along.'

I held her hands tightly in mine and implored her to take hold of herself. There was nobody waiting for her. She looked deep into my eyes and said: 'I am serious, *puttar*.' Then, after a pause, she continued, 'I want you to do me one last favour.'

I waited. After a brief pause she said: 'Go and meet Sardar Attar Singh of Amritsar. He will tell you why I have sent you to him.'

Attar Singh. I vaguely recalled a tall, very straight gentleman who had visited us occasionally in Lahore and been very kind to us. Nothing more.

'Why should I go and meet him?' I asked.

Why indeed? I wanted to know. That was my second question that elicited no answer. By then she had again become incoherent. Her face was flushed and her brow was hot. She had run out of breath and her breast heaved laboriously. I waited patiently for her breathing to normalise. But she drifted into a deep sleep never to wake up from. As

I sat by her bedside, waiting for her to complete the story, she was transported to another world where there was no pain, no mortal sorrow.

She left me behind with a host of questions that no one could or would answer. Not her husband, my taciturn baba, who wrapped himself in a shroud of silence and refused to speak once bibi's body was carried out of the house; not my siblings, who would not know the meaning of my last conversation with bibi; nobody who could shed light on what bibi wanted to tell me in her last gasps. All that she gave me was a clue pointing towards Amritsar and there I was, within days of bibi's funeral and *antim ardas*, finding my way through Attar ka Katra in the holy city of Amritsar, knocking with temerity at the door of Sardar Attar Singh. What would I say to him? How would I explain my unannounced appearance? I had no clue. But there I was.

Sardar Attar Singh was not at home when I knocked on the metal-studded door of his imposing house in Amritsar. There were three young children – two boys and a girl – aged between five and ten, running about the courtyard. Seeing me they scurried in to call their mother. A young well-rounded woman, probably in her late twenties, came out and received me with polite civility but when I introduced myself her attitude changed. Her mouth opened wide in an unuttered exclamation, her eyes widened with astonishment, and she got up from her seat, came up to me and embraced me lightly.

'*Puttar*, how you have grown, my child,' she said, much to my astonishment for she did not seem much older than me, certainly not old enough to be my mother. So why was she calling me *puttar*?

Seeing the surprised look on my face, she continued: 'You are like my son. After all Sardar sahib's son is my son, too. I have no grudges against you.'

Grudges? Sardar sahib's son? Perhaps she meant my baba. Was she then baba's sister? I did not quite understand but I remained silent, waiting for her to enlighten me. Seeing the void look on my face she continued, 'But never mind, we can talk about it later,' and hastened to make me comfortable.

By the time Sardar Attar Singh returned home I had bathed and changed, eaten a hearty meal and was relaxing in a room that apparently belonged to the two boys I had seen in the courtyard. They were Attar Singh's sons, Bantu and Bablu. Sprightly little fellows with little handkerchief covered *joodas* on the top of their heads, they were much younger than I. I found it difficult to make friends with them, so I restricted my conversation to monosyllables uttered only when a question was directed at me. Their mother instructed them to call me veer-ji with due respect. Big brother – that was a new one for me, accustomed as I was to being the youngest in Lahore.

Even before Attar Singh entered the house the children surrounded him at the entrance, excitedly telling him of veer-ji's arrival. Their mother joined them. Breaking away from the clamour of voices, he came forward to greet me. He was tall and elegant. In his hand he carried a riding whip that told me of his horseback journey back home. He walked up, caught me by the shoulders, looked at me directly in the face and smiled. It was a warm smile that made me feel immediately at home. A smile that began at his lips and ended in his eyes which twinkled with generosity and affection.

'*Puttar*, you have come from Lahore,' it was more of a statement than a question.

'Yes,' I responded briefly. Suddenly I had the feeling that words were not needed. This man facing me knew what I was here for. He understood me. He was mine. But what was this inexplicable bond between him and me? I searched in those deep-set eyes, the aquiline nose and the greying beard but could not find any clues that would help me arrive at a satisfactory solution to the mystery that bogged me down. Was he reading my thoughts? He patted me on the shoulder and told me we would have plenty of time for conversation, and went in to wash and change. His wife hurried into the kitchen to get his meal ready.

That night, after dinner, knowing that I wished to talk to Attar Singh, the lady of the house excused herself and went in to pack the children off to bed, leaving me alone with my host.

I told Attar Singh about bibi's demise and her dying instructions. He listened carefully and when I had finished, remained silent for a long time, as though unsure of what to say. I waited for him to break the silence. We were sitting in the *baithak* where guests were normally entertained. Now that the children and their mother had gone to sleep, the distant snatch of voices had also faded away. Attar Singh and I were wide awake and silent.

After a while he got up and went into the adjoining study, telling me to follow. There he opened a cupboard and the locker inside it. Taking out something wrapped in a blue silk cloth, he motioned me towards the writing desk in the corner. Placing the object on the table, he removed the cloth to lay bare an ivory-inlaid carved wooden box. This he opened slowly as I watched.

Inside the box were a few assorted items: some official looking papers tied up with a string, a leather-bound red notebook and something wrapped in coloured paper. He removed the paper to reveal a large shining red stone. The stone glinted in the light of the lamp, casting multicoloured hues all around. He held it up in the hollow of his palm and I noted that it was part of a brooch, a jewel that could be pinned to a dress.

Placing it back in the box, Attar Singh then handed me the diary, the bundle of papers and the notebook, saying, 'Here lies the answer to the questions in your heart. I guess this is what you are seeking.'

I remained silent, fascinated by the jewel which flashed and glinted in the dull light of the lamp. Picking up the stone I examined it closely. Although I was ignorant about precious stones it was obvious that this was a very valuable one. The light it emitted spoke for itself.

Then I thumbed the notebook. It was a dateless diary filled with a large spidery hand that seemed to be a woman's. I turned the pages at random. There were exclamations, marginal notes and doodles, drawings and random poems, along with lengthy, closely written text. A quick glance at the loose papers tied together revealed that they were some certificates, official records, a telegram, and some letters with remnants of broken seals still sticking to them.

'What's this?' I asked.

'Answers to your questions, my dear,' said Attar Singh briefly with a sigh.

'What do I do with these?'

Again he read my thoughts. 'Take them. They belong to you. They will answer all your questions and also acquaint you with facts you are unfamiliar with.'

I idly turned the leaves of the diary in my hand without really registering what I saw or what he said. How did it all connect? The diary, the sheaf of papers, the jewel in the box, this tall man facing me, and I? What was the link between these disparate items?

He saw the consternation on my face, sighed, and said: 'Official records will tell you that you are my son from my first marriage.'

'What?' I almost shouted.

This was unexpected, to say the least, especially the way he said it – without emotion, in a nonchalant, matter-of-fact manner.

'Are you serious?' I asked.

He said nothing. Just smiled.

'And the lady ...' I pointed towards the room where Attar Singh's wife had retreated for the night.

'She is my second wife.'

'My first wife died in childbirth,' he added nonchalantly.

'And you mean to say I am the child ...?' I stammered again.

'Well, again, records will tell you that you are the child she died giving birth to,' he said evasively. 'But ...,' he continued after a pause, 'the reality is known to just a handful of people. And very soon it will be known to you as well. The contents of this box here will shed some light on the truth. It will tell you whatever I know. And I certainly do not claim to know all.'

I had thought that Attar Singh was the end of my journey. When I had knocked at his gate earlier during the day, I had imagined that I was close to the object of my quest but now I realised that it was not the end but the beginning of a quest. I saw the answers to my unasked questions eluding my grasp, floating like autumn leaves in a dust storm, flying into my face and blinding me with the suddenness of their impact.

We sat down near the *angeethi* burning in the corner and began a long conversation that ended only in the wee hours of the morning when we heard the cock crowing somewhere in the backyard. I sat with the diary and the jewel in my lap, listening intently to the unbelievable story coming out of Attar Singh's mouth in a slow, staccato fashion but I could not grasp much. It was too sudden and too confusing for me to comprehend fully. What I did gather was that baba and bibi were not my real parents; they had taken on the role of parents when I was just a baby. At the same time, Attar Singh's remark that I was his son 'only on paper' confused me even more.

Several times, as Attar Singh narrated the story, I had the suspicion that I was dreaming. Or perhaps my host was rambling – he did have a faraway look in his eyes. All the same, some disjointed revelations did make an impact in my mind. Bibi had brought me up like her own son. I had never suspected that I was not her flesh and blood for there was no difference at all in her treatment of me and my siblings – rather my cousins.

Then Attar Singh began to narrate a story which I was least prepared for. It was the kind of story one read about in fairy tales. The kind one would encounter in classical mythology – with protagonists like Oedipus Rex or Paris or Hercules, or whatever. I had often heard such fantastic, out-of-the ordinary narratives but never had I given credence to them. This one, however, seemed to touch me intimately. Half in disbelief, I sat silently, listening to him.

A bejewelled king in shining robes on a sleek dark horse, a beautiful, fair maiden with flashing eyes and blonde hair. A dreamy city on a mountain top. Tall trees, winding roads, music and laughter in a magical sky. Wafting clouds and whispering winds. An elopement, hue and cry, excitement, suspense, thrill. Followed by pain, sorrow, intrigue and death. It was all there in his narrative.

It comes back to me today on the ridge, as I sit resting my back against the stone walls of the parapet overlooking the valley. I go back to that night in Amritsar, the story that came to me through the dog-eared pages of the red leather-bound notebook, and fragments of the tale narrated by Attar Singh. With the early winter chill nipping at my ears, I hear the murmur of his voice again. It mingles with the wind whistling through my hair, chanting songs of a time that was. Of lives once lived. Here on this mountain top, in a time gone by.

RAJEN

SUMMER FROLICS

Simla, October 1892

The sun had set several hours ago on the far side of the western range but the night was still young. There was a nip in the air and the two sentries pacing up and down the ridge quickened their pace, trying to keep themselves warm. The durbans at the main entrance of Gaiety Theatre stood motionless at their post. A mischievous breeze lifted the helm of their frock-coats and rustled the fantail turbans on their heads. They remained unperturbed, staring vacantly into the distance.

The sentries parading outside the church were aware that nothing untoward would take place in their vicinity that night. So were the patrolling horsemen outside the Town Hall. Tomorrow, perhaps things would liven up again in this area but tonight it was the viceroy's hill that commanded all attention.

In the distance, perched gaily atop the hill about three kilometres away, was the Viceregal Lodge, lit up in all its splendour. While the ridge was deserted and Gaiety Theatre too wore a desolate look, the Viceregal Lodge was the hub of all activity on this particular day. It was yet another Friday Night Ball in British Simla. The viceroy and his wife were hosting their weekly party and the entire population of the little hill town was gathered there. That was the hub of all action on this particular night.

The bushes around the Viceregal Lodge wore a festive look, lit up with small light bulbs. The sahib *log* were inside with the memsahibs. Sounds of laughter could be heard every time the doors opened to receive yet another important guest. The lilt of happy voices, the tinkle of glasses, along with the strains of the 'Blue Danube' played by the band, wafted through the otherwise silent night. Outside it was chilly and dark but under the bright chandelier lights within, elegant couples glided back and forth on the dance floor. The swish of gowns and the click of heels, the curtsey and the bow, the foxtrot and the waltz completed the scene. The hostess had ensured that all the lights of the building were switched on, some bright, some muted. She was happily engaged in zealous experimentation with new-found electricity. In addition, lighted candles were strategically placed in alcoves and corners.

Those Friday Night Balls were the talk of the town. Everyone who was someone made it a point to be present. The white population of the summer capital was there in toto. Some single, some with families, some women and children but not many men who, incidentally, were on duty in the sweltering heat of the plains. Their young wives, half-seriously called grass widows, would not miss out on the much-awaited social gathering and made it a point to attend the Friday specials. Some Indians, too, were invited – those who were close to the Englishmen, or who worked in tandem with them. And some were invited from the royal houses of Patiala, Kapurthala and Deeg – young rulers towards whom the British were favourably inclined and who were popular with the white gentry.

Rajinder Singh came into the last category. As the present Maharaja of Patiala he commanded a grudging respect from the white colonisers. They needed his support to control the turbulent hot-blooded Punjabis. Barely out of his teens, he was the darling of his people, the suave leader the masses looked up to, the dashing horseman, the popular icon, their hero, their bridge between the East and the West. Without doubt, he was the blue-eyed boy, born with a silver spoon. Rajinder Singh was there too at the Friday Ball. With a presence that could not be ignored, he was always the centre of attention and the much sought for guest at every party. They all agreed that he was indeed royalty personified, every little inch a maharaja.

Back in Patiala, Rajinder Singh was held in awe not just because he was the ruler but because he towered above everyone else in more ways than one. He had several advantages, some that he was born with, others that he acquired. For instance, he had the tall, imposing physique of his grandfather, the Late Maharaja Sir Narendra Singh. The *Sir* in the title announced loud and clear the cordial relations Patiala maintained with the British. Patiala was accepted as a nineteen-gun salute state. This was the legacy inherited by his successors.

Rajinder Singh, the present maharaja, had also inherited his father's gentle mannerism; the urbane polish, the chivalric demeanour and the sophistication that won many a female heart. It was easy to see in him the reflection of his late father of whom he had only vague memories. Maharaja Sir Mahendra Singh had died when his son and heir was barely four years old. They said it was a natural death but Rajen (as Rajinder Singh was popularly called) had heard rumours to the contrary. The age of twenty-four was no age for a 'natural' death. Rajen had often chanced upon hushed conversation which would die out as soon as he came into the room. He was not unaware of the strange looks exchanged among the grown-ups whenever his father's demise was inadvertently mentioned. Rajen noted it all but pretended to be ignorant for they were all good to him, servants, relatives, and immediate family, all of them bent over backward trying to please him. He loved this feeling of being treated as special, as the royal benefactor, the head of the palace.

Born on 25 May 1872, Rajen was crowned the ruler of the princely state when he was just four years old. According to the prevalent rules, it had to be this way. As early as 1859, the heads of the three Phulkian States, Nabha, Patiala, and Jind, had submitted a 'Paper of Requests' to the British government, that in the event of a minor succeeding as heir to the throne of any of the three states, the charge of administration should be entrusted to a Council of Regency comprising three able and trustworthy officials of the state selected by the British government and in consultation with the other two surviving Phulkian chiefs. In such circumstances, the British agent, that is, the commissioner, took on the responsibility of the proper grooming of the minor, looking after his upbringing and education. The British had acceded to this Paper of Requests according to the Sanad of 1860. Consequently, their relations with the Phulkian states had remained cordial, particularly after the 1857 uprising, when the Phulkian chiefs had remained loyal to the British rulers. In return, they gained greater concessions and autonomy in their day-to-day governance.

The coronation of the minor successor was a solemn affair. A mini-size turban studded with diamonds was placed on Rajen's head with a string of pearls around his neck. He was dressed in an *achkan* of gold brocade with matching trousers and gilded Patiala *juttis*. An ornate sword was slung across his waist. It was a proper, full-sized sword, so heavy that he almost staggered under its weight. But ceremonies had to be conducted and Rajen had stoically braved the ordeal. He was to remain the maharaja from 1876 to his death. During the first fourteen years, from 1876 to 1890, when he attained maturity, the affairs of the state were managed by the rajmata, Maharani Mai Sahib, with the help of a Council of Regency. When he came of age in 1890, he was invested with full powers by the then viceroy of India, Lord Lansdowne.

While he awaited his turn to the throne, Rajinder Singh was given conventional education like any young boy of the times along with the special education considered fit for the throne. He was trained in martial arts, horse-riding, and polo. That was a time when *vilayati* education was a must for someone of his status, so they sent him to England. After all, as the ruler of an Indian state he had to be well-equipped for his interaction with the British. His predecessors had maintained cordial ties with them and he would certainly not be found wanting. Rajen was educated at Cambridge, England, where he studied the British system of government. On his return to Patiala this knowledge came in handy and he set up free hospitals for women, orphanages, and other philanthropic institutions in his princely state. He came to be regarded as a just and enlightened ruler.

In England, Rajen was something of a curiosity. Because of his royal patronage he was treated as a special guest of the queen, introduced to all the lords who thronged Buckingham Palace, and soon became a part of all their official meetings concerning India. Socially, too, his popularity grew and he was invited to their parties where he learned the art of elegantly raising a toast to his gracious hosts. Without doubt, he was accepted as one of them. In particular, the young women at the parties were fascinated by him. He travelled through Europe and absorbed all that he saw and heard.

Rajen was a voracious reader. When he was not horse-riding or playing polo, he was reading poetry. Edward Fitzgerald's translation of Omar Khayyam in particular appealed to him as did the great Romantic poets, Tennyson and Browning. He lapped them all up eagerly, memorised verses to impress the young female admirers who surrounded him at parties. He was the life of every social activity and he enjoyed it to the hilt. What intrigued him the most was the attention he received from the women at Hampton Court. They would swish into the ballroom with their gowns trailing behind them, escorted by handsome young men. Some younger ones came escorted by ageing matriarchs. The women loved him just as much as he loved their company. Although he was young in years, they knew he was royalty, even if the royalty belonged to another part of the world. He was exotic. He was intriguing.

Some relationships grew stronger, even intimate. But Rajen never forgot that he would have to return to his country one day. Although he was infatuated by white skin and blonde hair many a time, he avoided all serious commitment.

In any case, stronger than his infatuation for English women was his passion for horses and motorcars. Cars and horses, horses and cars: they fascinated him. In particular, he was taken up by the Deboin Bouton, the French car that was then particularly in vogue. He was determined that one day he would be the proud owner of that beauty – he would take it home with him to Patiala. Sure enough, his dream came true in 1892. When he returned to India, behind him rolled in the four-wheeled beauty, its engine purring softly. Another unusual souvenir that he brought along was equestrian – an extraordinary Irish stud, sleek and dark, that he named Sultan.

Rajen had finally come of age so he was invested with full ruling powers and became the de facto ruler. The whole city state of Patiala seemed to rejoice on the occasion. People came out in the streets, crowded on rooftops, hung from the trees, jostled and pushed to get a glimpse of their new debonair maharaja. He was now the confirmed ruler of the nineteen-gun salute princely state and savoured every moment of his glory as his cavalcade made its way out of the Moti Bagh Palace, through the Baradari gardens into the city. He looked around at the cheering crowds and waved from his car. His people loved him and he was also in the good books of the British. They knew him as a fearless rider, an excellent shooter, an ace cricketer, and a fine billiard player. All these attributes endeared him to the imperial power and he found it easy to establish a rapport with them.

But Patiala came first. Rajen had big plans for the royal state. He was determined that under his leadership it would emerge as the foremost state of the country, not just politically but holistically. With the help of his English friends he would transform the lives of his people. Even as he was being anointed he had dreams of setting up a community centre in the Baradari Gardens with huge polo grounds, a gymnasium and other recreation facilities. He would also set up world-class educational institutions, a medical college, perhaps, for his people. His father had been instrumental in establishing the Mahendra College and he must continue the legacy.

He continued to be passionate about cricket and polo. Soon he earned the reputation of being the best polo player in India, as well as one of the finest cricketers and billiard players of his day. The Baradari, the Moti Bagh Palace grounds, and the Rajindra Club precincts, all became practice grounds for his interests and he encouraged his men to get on to the field with him as soon as the day's work was done. Helping him in these arts which he had learned in England was his trusted friend, Charles Bryan. From England along with Sultan, the splendid Irish horse, he had also imported an Irish horse trainer. Charles Bryan was to be the master of the stables in Patiala.

Rajen had met Charles first in England; it was their passion for horses that had brought them together. Then a middle-rung cavalry officer in Her Majesty Queen Victoria's service, it was Charles who introduced Rajen to fashionable London pastimes like horse-racing and polo. He was much older than Rajen but on a special request from Lord Curzon, the then viceroy of India, he had agreed to play host to the young maharaja on his London visit. He deemed it his duty to initiate him into the social customs of England, the etiquette, the proprieties of polite interaction, and all that makes one a desirable social animal. Charles was given to understand that a proper grooming of the maharaja was essential and would ensure cordial relations between the ruling British government in India and the princely state of Patiala, so he spared no effort in familiarising the young prince with the proprieties of English social customs.

With Charles and his wife, Minnie Bryan, Rajen enjoyed a reciprocal warm relationship. So thick grew their friendship that when Rajen had to return to India he requested Charles to come along with him. It was an unusual request and needed much persuasion but Rajen was not in the habit of being turned down. He tried various ways of coaxing him and finally succeeded when he managed to convince Charles that he would be given an almost royal treatment in Patiala, with facilities appropriate for the first officer of the state.

This is how Charles and Minnie Bryan found themselves in India. They had a daughter, too, the young Florence. Florence had a delicate constitution and had recently recovered from a severe respiratory disease. The family doctor had advised them not to subject her frail constitution to the heat and dust of the Indian subcontinent. Perhaps later, when she regained her strength she could join them if she so wished. Thus, it was that Florence stayed behind with her cousins in the custody of her maternal aunt when Charles and Minnie accompanied Rajen back to India.

In Patiala, the Bryans made their home in a separate wing of the palace allotted to them by the maharaja. Charles supervised the polo grounds and the stables, ensuring that the royal horses were kept in good shape. Common interests and a mutual trust nurtured and strengthened the bond between them. The newly acquired wonder car from France was also under his care. Although formally Rajen was Charles's employer, they were more like friends. When not dealing with the affairs of the state, the maharaja was always in the Bryans' company. Minnie was an excellent hostess and provided the best of snacks when they sat together in the evening over a bottle of the finest scotch whisky. There was always a large retinue of available servants but Minnie made it a point to attend on them personally. Rajen loved her for that.

The British were not too happy about the relationship. For how could a white man, a subject of Her Majesty, be in the employ of a vassal state? It did not seem right. However, because of the personal charm of the ruler of Patiala, and because of the cordial relations between the two ruling powers, it was prudent to turn a blind eye to this aberration. Rajen, the very westernised, very popular, very avant-garde Sikh ruler of the virulent Punjabis, was a good friend to have and an excellent party animal. A perfect bridge between the East and the West. For this reason he was an almost permanent invitee at the viceregal balls in the Simla hills.

For this particular party Rajen had galloped on horseback all the way to Simla. He would have loved to drive up in his new motor car but knowing that it would not be possible – the roads were narrow and winding, the journey arduous, and the car may come to a standstill en route – he decided to go riding, the way he usually did. The distance from Patiala to Simla was formidable but Rajen had made it in little more than half a day. Charles Bryan had made all the necessary preparations, given him the best of the royal steeds, organised horse-changing at stations on the way, and a posse of soldiers to accompany him.

The Viceregal Lodge was a huge structure spread over an entire hill. The main building was big enough to house all the guests who attended the parties. They would come from the city area in their horse-driven carts, or sometimes in coolie-rickshaws, and stay on through the night at the viceroy's lodge. When the ball ended in the wee hours of the morning, they would return home, still dazed with the wines and the champagnes that flowed freely. Sometimes, the following morning too was an extension of revelry, with all the young men and women riding off into the woods for a picnic, accompanied by servants carrying loads of food and drink. Courtships and secret liaisons had plenty of opportunity to flourish in the given circumstances. Then there were also the horse races, romance and adventure, thrill and excitement, all in a heady mix that pervaded the hillside.

For Rajen, this particular Friday night was of special importance. At the last ball he had espied Betty, the viceroy's daughter who had recently arrived from London. Betty, frail, white and vivacious, had bewitched the maharaja and he had thought of nothing else but her deep blue eyes with the hint of mischief in them, her golden ringlets, and her ivory white skin. Ever since that last ball when he had first set eyes on her, Betty, Betty, and Betty it was who haunted his dreams with her lilting laugh and the small red mouth like a half-blown rosebud. But Betty was always surrounded by many. Her governess and her mother, the viceroy's wife, were always in the vicinity, so Rajen knew he would have to devise some other way of getting her sole attention.

The thought of Betty excited him; he brandished his whip and spurred his horse, trying to get to his destination at the earliest possible. Usually it took him a whole day to reach Simla but on this particular day he had made it even before sunset. He had reached the viceroy's lodge well before the party. His horses were taken to the stables and he was shown his rooms where he could freshen up and relax before the guests came in.

Relaxation was the last thing on his mind. Betty, where was Betty? He knew he would have to bide his time as she would not appear before all the guests arrived. Rajen waited impatiently, cooling his heels.

Finally twilight took over. The tall trees around the mansion reverberated with the twitter of birds returning to their nests at the end of the day. Fireflies went peek-a-boo in the bushes and the hum of crickets could be heard in the garden when wheels finally started rolling up the driveway. Wheels of the buggies, the horse carts, the tongas, and the manually pulled coolie-rickshaws that brought in the guests. The regular churning of wheels on the narrow cart road was punctuated by the intermittent clang of rickshaw bells. Families from Dyerton, from Oakville, from Annandale, from beyond the ridge and the church rolled in. The young ladies in their fine dresses, the old matronly ones in all their staid, proper, sensible formal clothes, the children scrubbed clean, the young men in tall hats, tail-coats and shining boots. They all came either on wheels or on horseback, dismounted at the main entrance, and were ushered into the brightly lit hall amid excited chatter.

UNDER A SPANGLED SKY

The chandeliers winked merrily and split into a thousand different shards of light, dancing off the ornate wooden carved ceiling, twinkling over the framed portraits hanging on the walls, pausing a while on the mantelpiece before spilling over on to the dance floor. The brass band in the corner played a lilting number that Rajen was not familiar with but it made him feel light on his toes. As he entered the hallway he looked at his multiple reflections in the full-length mirrors lining the walls and he was pleased with the effect. His turban was well in place, with the ruby prominently displayed above his forehead. On either side of the ruby there was a double string of pearls that adorned the turban. His long brocade coat was buttoned at the neck and he wore several strings of pearls around his throat. Around his waist was a thick gold chain, twisted like a rope, held in place with an ornate buckle. His trousers were a matching gold as were the *juttis* on his feet. He looked resplendent. He could see that he looked 'every inch a maharaja' as they said. Six feet two inches tall, his complexion was a healthy pink. His moustache and beard were thick and dark, neatly rolled and tucked under the chin. A gold chain on his watch dangled from the pocket of his coat. Around his wrist he had a thick gold *kara*, a band of gold, very robust and solid. A topaz ring glinted on the index finger of his right hand and a sapphire on the third finger of the left hand.

Yes, he was a maharaja, no doubt. So the image screamed loud and clear, making him smile to himself. But would this image please the spirited Betty? That was a question that bothered him.

He looked around the ballroom. A few couples were beginning to sway on the dance floor. He could see his friend Jagatjit bowing low before a demure wispy creature in a blue gown. No, it was not Betty, a quick glance told him. Then where was she?

He looked around again and finally espied her laughing and talking amid a gaggle of young girls in the corner. She was there, looking ethereal. Her blonde hair was tied up high to reveal her long, slender neck. She wore a pale cream satin gown which highlighted the pale pink of her skin. Around her throat, on a black ribbon, she wore an emerald set in gold. Her appearance was demure but the look that flashed from her blue eyes was anything but docile. There was a strange wildness about them, a recklessness that Rajen could only feel, not explain. He could sense intuitively that something between him and the fair-haired girl was brewing, although no words had yet been spoken.

Before Rajen could cross the hall the band started playing 'Daisy Bell' and a titter ran through the young crowd. Evidently, it was a favourite song and they all itched to be on the dance floor. A young Englishman with freckled pink cheeks jumped up and bowed before Betty who in turn curtsied and followed him on to the dance floor. Rajen watched them dance to the peppy number, Betty flushed and out of breath, the young man lightly holding her by the waist, smiling into her face.

Rajen watched, clenching and unclenching his fist. But a polite smile did not once leave his face.

The dance over, Betty returned to her giggling group in the corner. A waiter approached her with a laden tray and she picked up a glass of lemonade. As she raised the glass to her lips she looked up and seemed to freeze. The glass half-way to her lips, her eyes wide open, still panting from the exercise on the dance floor, a thin film of perspiration on her forehead, she flushed when she saw Rajen towering above her. The ruby in his turban glinted and formed a pattern on her face as he bowed lightly from the waist and gently smiled.

Betty's consternation was only momentary. She regained her poise quickly and extended her right hand towards the dashing young maharaja who touched it lightly to his lips, smiling all the while.

The young girls of Betty's group suddenly seemed to melt away. Perhaps they had moved on to the dance floor. Or perhaps they had felt the palpable chemistry between the maharaja and their friend and thought it prudent to leave them alone.

Betty and Rajen stood under an archway, engaged in light conversation. Their eyes were locked and they were oblivious of the whirling couples around them. Towering above her petite frame, he looked deep into the fathomless blue eyes and saw in them a kindred soul waiting to be called forth while she, in wonderment, found herself totally mesmerised by his royal demeanour, his intense eyes, the glinting apparel he wore, and – above all – the attention with which he addressed her. Betty had never received so much admiration and that too from so royal a personage. She found herself yielding to his touch, hypnotised, spell-bound.

'Keep away from the Indians,' Betty's mother, the viceroy's wife, had often warned her. 'Especially those of the royal families. They are very charming but messing with them will lead to no good. Just keep away from them.'

But those warnings were nothing to her now. For Betty, on this particular night, there was only this fascinating turbaned man holding her right hand in his, unwilling to let it go. And there was this world of music around them, the rhythmic beat of drums, the organ, the pipes and the trumpets playing, the swish of gowns and the tap of boots in a cadenced succession.

'This one for me, lady,' said the maharaja in his baritone, looking deep into her eyes. He liked the way her eyes widened when he talked to her. He liked the way a small crease formed over the bridge of her nose when she laughed. He liked the oversized mole at the base of her neck, just above the pendant she wore. He wanted to touch it. Would she let him?

Betty blushed a deep red as though she had read his thoughts. With her ravishing beauty, she was used to such attention from her male admirers, but this one was different. When Rajen looked into her eyes she felt vulnerable. She felt weak in the knees. She could feel her heart hammering against her ribs. He had this curious effect on her.

Rising to her feet, she curtsied and allowed him to lead her to the dance floor. From the corner of her eye she could see heads turning and curious looks directed towards her but it did not seem to matter. She disregarded her governess, Mlle Berton, who kept a hawk's eye over her all the time and was now seated in the corner, keeping a watchful – and disapproving – vigil. She could sense her mother, talking to the viceroy at the far end of the room, turning to look at her with a vague sense of unease but, again, it did not matter. Rajen was in full control of the situation as they began swaying to the music. On popular request it was 'Daisy Bell' again:

Daisy, Daisy, give me your answer, do,
I'm half crazy all for the love of you.

It won't be a stylish marriage –
I can't afford a carriage
But you'd look sweet upon the seat
Of a bicycle built for two.

We will go tandem man and wife,
Daisy, Daisy,
Wheeling away down the road of life,
I and my Daisy Bell.
When the night's dark, we can both despise
Policemen and lamps as well.
There are bright lights in the dazzling eyes
Of beautiful Daisy Bell.

The music was lively and the floor was crowded. It was the kind of song that would make anyone get up and dance.

'Won't you come with me, my Daisy Bell?' he whispered in her ear.

Betty blushed and giggled. He repeated the question.

'But,' he said, modifying the lyrics of the song, 'I *can* afford a carriage and you will look very sweet in it, sitting beside me.'

Betty smiled, not knowing what to say.

He continued: 'If not the carriage, you could sit with me in my car. You know, the French Deboin Bouton. The only motorcar in this country.'

'Yes, I heard about it. I would love to ride in it!' gushed Betty.

As Rajen and Betty swayed to the music they were jostled from time to time by the other couples around them but they did not mind. Hemmed in by the crowds, they were forced to dance close. Betty was breathless and excited. She was quite sure her partner would be able to hear her heartbeat. Pressed close to him, she was transported to another world – a world different from the sheltered life she had lived so far. This was a world of reckless excitement, romance, adventure and love. She wanted to abandon herself to this new-found ecstasy, to the thrill that ran through her entire being when she felt the maharaja's breath, warm and sensuous, on her bare neck. Or when the string of pearls around his throat got entangled with the brooch on her shoulder. He had to pause in between the dance then, lean forward and gently separate the beads from the jewel. All the while her heart continued to beat wildly. She thought it would burst.

As they spun around to the music, he twirled her closer to the terrace. The doors were slightly ajar and a cool breeze wafted in.

'Let's get out of here,' he whispered in her ear. 'It's getting warm inside.'

She willingly allowed herself to be led on to the terrace. They stood looking down at the valley that fell steeply on the western side of the hill. It was a clear night and there was a bright full moon in the sky, surrounded by a million twinkling stars. They stood in a corner looking at the distant hills outlined against the sky. Rajen held Betty's hand lightly and spoke to her in soft, almost caressing tones. More like a murmur, she thought. The murmur of a gently flowing brook finding its way through a silent dark forest.

She was fascinated by the ruby on his turban which glinted in the moonlight.

'May I touch it?' she asked hesitantly.

'Of course,' he replied gallantly with a bow. 'It's yours. Take it.'

Unpinning it from the folds of his turban, he placed it in her palm and closed her fingers around the jewel.

'No,' she protested mildly. 'I did not mean that.'

'But I insist,' he replied and pinned it on her dress. 'I have another one with me here. And a much bigger jewel at home in Patiala – an emerald that radiates light. I will give it to you.'

'No, no,' again she protested.

'These jewels are meant for someone like you,' said he. 'You will enhance their worth.'

Removing one of the several strings of pearls that he wore, he placed it around her neck. As he straightened the strands she felt the soft touch of his palms on her skin.

'See how pretty it looks on you,' he said, his hands still resting lightly on her bare neck.

She was at a loss for words. All that she was aware of was the proximity of this young man who seemed to sweep her off her feet, in whose presence she felt she was losing herself. Floundering. Drowning. Sinking.

They remained motionless for a while. Then came a pause in the music from the dance hall. A round of applause and some cheering. A door in the far corner suddenly opened and a young couple came giggling on to the terrace, forcing them to jump apart.

Rajen, taken aback momentarily, soon regained his composure and began declaiming in a high pitch:

Oh moon – Art thou pale for weariness
  Of climbing heaven, and gazing on the earth,

Wandering companionless
Among the stars that have a different birth, –
And ever changing, like a joyous eye
That finds no object worth its constancy?
                    – P. B. Shelley, *To the Moon*

Betty, too, pulled herself together and responded: 'Oh, I love poetry.'

A semblance of normalcy returned to their conversation and they nodded genially to the couple that had joined them on the terrace. It was his friend Jagatjit Singh with the girl he was talking to earlier. A polite exchange of greetings and the two pairs moved to opposite corners of the terrace.

Betty and Rajen looked down from their corner at the garden below. It was laid out in terraces spread across the entire hill. Just below them Betty pointed out a sundial which could accurately show the time when the days were not cloudy. On a lower terrace was a row of fragrant rose bushes.

As they looked down together something moved below. A shadow emerged from the main building and went into the garden. Immediately after came another shadow in close pursuit. A rustle of silk followed by the click of boots. A suppressed giggle and then a throaty chuckle. The two shadows became one under the archway leading to the lower garden. The single shadow moved and swayed gently. Muted sounds of endearment mingled with soft sighs and moans and wafted up to the terrace with the breeze. Then the shadows began to descend the steps slowly, moving towards the far end of the lower garden and went out of sight behind the rambling roses.

Rajen and Betty stood watching in silence. Betty was somewhat uneasy and wanted to go back indoors but Rajen held her back.

'Meet me there later tonight,' Rajen whispered in Betty's ear.

An inner voice told Betty she should not but she found herself saying, 'I will'.

They turned to go back into the bright lights of the dance hall where couples were still dancing to another popular number:

> After the ball is over
> After the break of morn –
> After the dancers' leaving;
> After the stars are gone;
> Many a heart is aching,
> If you could read them all;
> Many the hopes that have vanished
> After the ball.

Apparently, their brief absence had not been noticed. Betty and Rajen again mingled with the partying crowd.

Two hours later, the moon having travelled across the sky, was still shining brightly, still surrounded by stars that continued to twinkle. The music in the hall still played on. Drinks still flowed freely. However, the chatter was somewhat subdued. High-pitched voices had given way to softer conversation. People had broken up into smaller groups engaged in serious discussion. Some were slumped in easy chairs, looking around vacantly, either inebriated or just drowsy. An overweight middle-aged man was seen fast asleep on a sofa in the corner, one arm slung over the armrest, his pipe fallen to the floor. A few dancers, however, still pirouetted to the music.

Outside, in the garden, Betty hurried down the terraced steps, wrapped up in a dark woollen shawl. She tiptoed past the sundial, avoiding the pool of light from the ballroom windows above. Close to the rose bushes she saw a dark shadow that could only be Rajen's.

He was waiting for her. As she approached he silently held out his hand. Together they walked to the far end of the garden leading to the terrace below. The sounds of the dance hall grew faint and Betty was aware of the overpowering silence of the mountains. She was also aware of the pounding of her heart. It was chilly and her breath came out in vapours. Rajen seemed to be in control of himself but when he spoke his voice was low and shaky.

'Thank you for coming, my princess. You have made me so happy.' He held her close.

Inadvertently she shivered and huddled against him. He led her to a stone bench in the corner overlooking the valley. There they sat for a long time, talking in low tones, murmuring to each other. As the moon gradually sank lower and lower, they continued to talk, pouring out their pent-up emotions accumulating from the time they had first set eyes on each other.

Time did not stand still. The moon continued its journey towards the horizon. The stars began to fade. The music indoors had long since died out. Before long, the lights would go out and the last of the revellers would retire to their rooms. Soon the sky too would begin to change colour. Rajen and Betty knew they did not have much time. Dreading the moment when they were to part, they sat on the stone bench, unmindful of the gathering chill, of the dew that settled on them, of the uncomfortable, cold seat.

And suddenly Rajen forced the question: 'Why don't you come with me to my palace?'

'Huh?' Betty was taken by surprise. He repeated the question.

'Why don't you come with me to Patiala? Be my queen. I want you to be mine. Mine forever.'

Was it the moonlight or was it the smell of jasmine in the air that made him say that? Betty would never know. She did not answer.

He addressed her again: 'I know that you care for me the way I care for you. Tell me, don't you?'

She did not answer. Her heart screamed, 'Yes, yes, I do'. But her lips remained sealed.

He needed no answer. The look in her eyes was enough.

'Marry me, Betty,' and he knelt at her feet.

Something snapped within her. She gasped. All her life she had dreamed of a handsome young man in shining armour kneeling at her feet, asking for her hand. And here was this dream turning into reality. She pinched herself and felt the pain. Yes, it was for real!

'But ... but ... ,' she stuttered and could not go on.

He guessed her thoughts again.

'You hesitate because I am not one of you? But I understand you. I love you, my dear. I will keep you happy.'

'But you already have a ... a ... .'

'Yes,' he sighed. 'I do have a wife in Patiala. But you will be my favourite queen. I will build another palace for you.

Our children will be royal heirs. Our son will be a prince and have the right of succession after me.'

Inundated, deluged, overpowered by a host of unfamiliar feelings, Betty still hesitated.

'Come on, Betty. You know I will keep you happy. You will not miss your people. When they know how much we love each other they will relent. I will bring your mother and father around.'

He had risen to his feet and was bending over her, her face cupped in his palms. All she was aware of was the face looming above hers. The sky whirled around, the tall deodar trees moved in a slow circle, and the rose bushes seemed to rise and close in on her. She saw the earnest look in his eyes and found herself succumbing to his pleas. She shut her eyes and took a deep breath.

'Yes,' continued Rajen, still holding her close, compelling her to look at him. 'You will come with me to my palace.'

The words sank into her consciousness. He continued: 'I will leave now but I will wait for you at the ridge, near Gaiety Theatre at noon. You will not fail me. Come to me, my dearest, and we will fly from this place and make a haven for ourselves.'

A promise made, it was now time to part. Rajen and Betty quietly entered the main building again. She tiptoed upstairs to her room while he turned down the hallway towards the guest rooms. A few hours before the sun climbed over the horizon again. A few hours of sleep, if possible. And then the rendezvous at the ridge.

VIGIL AT THE RIDGE

The imperial summer capital was never an early riser. The few hundred odd dwelling units dotting the hillside were still enveloped in an early morning stupor when Rajen trotted down Cart Road and up the ridge on his black steed. His posse of horsemen was left below, near the clock tower and he rode up alone. Dismounting, he patted Sultan, his sleek dark horse, and tied it to a railing facing the church. He strolled to the eastern edge of the maidan and looked down. This was Mount Olympus of the ruling power, this 'Chhota Vilayat' or 'Little England' comprising these scattered houses dotting the hillside. This was their home away from home, their cure for nostalgia and home-sickness. In broad daylight it seemed almost ordinary, with its buildings of grey stone-and-wood façade but at sunset the unexplained charm of the hillside would return with the mystical hues of the setting sun, the changing colours of the sky, and the different tints and shades of the many ranges of hills visible along the horizon. Closer home, the clusters of twinkling lights across the hillside, demarcating the quarters of the local population in the Lower Bazaar area, and the more isolated brighter illumination in the bigger homes of the English officers would make it look like one huge Christmas tree. There was something in the location, the ambience and the very air that had the power to enchant. The magic of this place never ceased to fascinate Rajen; it was this magic that brought him back from Patiala every now and then.

At the ridge this morning, Rajen was not in the party clothes he had worn the night before. Today he was in his riding outfit: a deep red riding jacket trimmed with white at the throat and the cuffs, white riding breeches, tall tan knee-length boots with spurs, a whip in his right hand. In the other hand he held his riding gloves. The white turban on his head had a jewel glinting on it but no strings of pearls. Carelessly thrown over his shoulder was a dark woollen cape that fell to his knees. He walked up and down the length of the ridge, shoulders pushed back, his head held high. There was something regal about his gait, something magnetic about him which drew admiring glances from all the passers-by as he paced to and fro restlessly.

It was almost noon and although there was a bright sun above, he knew how treacherous Simla weather could be. Any time the sky could cloud over and it would begin to rain. He had a long ride ahead and it was not advisable to delay. But where was Betty? There was no sign of her.

The Mall below was beginning to get populated. It was time for a change of guard. A pair of British soldiers rode up to the ridge and relieved their counterparts. The durbans at Gaiety Theatre also changed duties. A few perambulators rolled up the Mall carrying pink-cheeked, blue-eyed chubby children, pushed by nannies and 'ayahs'. There were few local people around; the road was very much a European preserve and ill-dressed Indians were generally not allowed; however, they were free to use the Lower Mall. As Rajen looked around idly, three young girls almost identically dressed in tight jackets buttoned over long frocks, alighted from a horse-driven buggy outside the church. Behind them, in all probability escorting them, was another buggy with two older women in it. Their chaperones, presumably. Rajen could not see the faces of the young girls as they were turned away from him. The chaperones quickly ushered their wards inside the church.

The church was a popular destination on weekends. Dominating the landscape, it had stood its ground for almost seven decades. Reading the inscription on the door, Rajen saw that it had come up after December 1822 when Col. Boileau and Bengal Engineers had landed in Simla. It was the second church in North India. Where was the first? He wondered.

Strolling to the other side of the ridge, he looked at the Viceregal Lodge in the distance. Crowning the hill, with its tentacles spread in all directions, the building looked imposing and even forbidding. Suddenly a doubt rose in his mind and Rajen wondered if he would ever go up that hill again. Then, dismissing his thoughts as unfounded, he shook his head and continued promenading up and down the ridge.

As the sun rose higher and the mist evaporated, more and more people could be seen on the Mall. Some families, enjoying the weather, were loitering around, heading towards Gaiety. A few young men hanging out alone near the Town Hall and around the church seemed to be simply killing time. Perhaps they too, thought Rajen, had secret appointments and were looking forward to romantic encounters.

The church bells started tolling. It was now midday and Betty was still nowhere to be seen. Rajen knew he could not linger on much longer. He had to ride down to the plains. His posse was waiting for him. There was a long, arduous journey ahead.

He untied his horse and mounted it slowly. This was it. She was not going to come. And yet, last night – no, just a few hours ago – she had promised … . He sighed heavily as he tugged at his rein, turning Sultan away from the church.

As his horse began trotting slowly downhill, Rajen heard the sound of running feet. Looking back towards the church, he saw one of the three girls, who had earlier dismounted from the carriage, running towards his horse. She was wearing a low-brimmed hat and had a veil covering the lower half of her face but he knew it was Betty. Betty was calling out and running towards him, her long dress hitched up so that she would not trip. His heart missed a beat: yes, Betty it was. She had kept her promise.

Rajen, who had already come a few yards down the ridge to the fork touching the Mall near the Town Hall, turned his horse around and cantered back towards her. Still astride the horse, leaning over as she neared, he swooped down and picked her up with one easy sweep of his arm. The veil fell from her face and Betty, with her golden hair streaming under the low brimmed hat, her dress flying way up to her knees, found herself side-saddle on the horse with Rajen holding her tight.

This is how the strollers on the Mall saw Betty. Hearing the sudden commotion, they paused momentarily and looked around wondering what was happening. Mouth agape, they stood hypnotised by the vision of the sleek black horse, the fair, golden-haired damsel and the tall, dazzling, turbaned rider who held his prize tight, tugged at his reins and galloped down the hill before they could draw another breath. This is how eyewitnesses later recalled the fleeting image of the runaway couple. It was an extraordinary, ephemeral image that passed them like a vision in a split second. So swift was the vision that after describing it a few times they were unsure whether they could really believe what their eyes had seen. Did it really take place or had they imagined it?

Whether it was imagined or real, there was no denying that the story of the runaway couple made that spot immortal; that point at the juncture of four roads acquired a distinct identity. It became a landmark called *Scandal Point* although the story connected to it acquired several dimensions and grew misty with time. So much so, that if one asked the local people – What scandal? Or which scandal? – one would probably get as many answers as the number of people questioned. The event was no longer remembered as factual. It passed into the realm of myth and legend. All that the people of Simla remembered was some vague story about an English woman and a maharaja. Which English woman? Some said it was the viceroy's daughter, others thought it was his niece; still others believed it was just a white woman with no political connection. And if they were asked – which maharaja? – again there were contradictory responses. The *paan-wala* who had his little shop in the Lower Bazaar was convinced it was Maharaja Bhupinder Singh of Patiala, the old woman who took her morning walk regularly on the ridge believed it was Maharaja Rajinder Singh, and the young waiter at Hotel Dalziel who said his grandfather had actually seen the couple ride away, felt that it was the Maharaja of Kapurthala. Nobody had any clarity on the 'who' and 'why' of the event.

As time moved on they began to treat it like the countless tales associated with the hills, stories that drift through the consciousness, like the floating feathery clouds over the Mall and over the ridge, weaving in and out through the crowds of holiday-makers and pleasure-seekers: clouds so real that you feel you could almost touch them; but when you reach out they drift away leaving you empty-handed. And yet, like the clouds, the story continued to hover over the scene forever after.

Despite the lack of tangible relevant facts, despite any evidence to corroborate the story of the elopement, Scandal Point became a concrete landmark of the hill station. Right in the centre of the place where the four roads converged, a police post was constructed – a raised platform with an umbrella-type rain shelter – and it came to be accepted as a marker, a meeting ground for ramblers on the Mall and the ridge. This was the permanent legacy of the fairy tale that was otherwise consigned to the sphere of fantasy.

The Mall and the ridge continued to be the central hub of the town: the church retained its sanctity; Gaiety Theatre maintained its social importance as the focal point of cultural activity with occasional special performances for visiting dignitaries. On festivals there were floral decorations as usual, with garlands and bouquets, a cleaning up of the streets and a sense of excitement pervading the air. Simla, with its natural beauty, continued to reign supreme as the Queen of the Himachal for the next half-century and even after the white colonisers returned to the English Isles; the Viceregal Lodge continued to be the official residence of the English viceroy until 1947 when it was taken over by the Indian government and was rechristened as Rashtrapati Niwas. Soon after, Lala Lajpat Rai's statue was a post-independence addition to Scandal Point. Even to this day the freedom fighter looms large on the scene, looking at the police post sternly as though in disapproval of the story linked to the spot.

THE ROYAL CITY

As the horse with two riders galloped down the hill, coolie rickshaws labouring uphill, clanging their hand-bells, cleared the way for them in alarm. Rajen's horsemen, who had been waiting patiently all morning, heard the noisy clatter of hoofs and immediately became alert; mounting their horses again, they were ready to escort him as soon as his horse caught up with them. With two of his horsemen leading the royal stud and three bringing up the rear, Rajen and Betty galloped out of Simla as fast as they could, leaving behind nothing but a cloud of dust. Their horses were swift but they were in a hurry. Rajen knew he would have to reach safe ground before the viceroy's men set out in search of them. Within minutes they had left the Simla hills behind and did not stop until they reached Kandaghat. Here they halted briefly and changed horses, took a buggy for Betty and continued their downward journey. Patiala was still far off but their progress was good and they hoped to reach before sundown.

From Kandaghat Rajen dispatched a messenger with a missive for Charles Bryan, explaining the situation to him, asking him to make appropriate arrangements to receive the new maharani. He knew he could trust the man. It would not be easy, he knew. The senior maharani, Jasmer Kaur would not take it without a fight but Charles and Minnie Bryan would handle it. Of this he was certain.

Charles Bryan was a worried man. He was older than his young friend and master, the maharaja. And wiser too. In his wisdom he knew that there were troubled times ahead. He received the maharaja's message and sank into his chair, lost in deep thought. This is how his wife, Minnie, found him an hour later. Realising there was something serious troubling him, she drew up another chair close to him and addressed him softly.

'What is it Charles?'

'The maharaja,' he said, mopping the sweat of his brow.

'What's he done now?'

'He is bringing along an English woman as his maharani.' Charles's nose had turned a bright red, the way it did when he was under pressure. Beads of sweat glistened on his balding crown.

'Jesus Christ! This is serious! What do we do?' asked Minnie.

'If the word spreads it would mean trouble with the British. We have to counter that. The maharani, too, is in the palace – she would not take it lightly. You know how strong-willed she is.'

'What do we do?' Minnie repeated.

Charles sighed: 'I wish I knew.'

They sat in silence for a while. Then Minnie walked to the bar to fix some drinks. Bringing back two glasses on a tray, she saw Charles still in deep thought, his eyes shut, and a frown creasing his forehead.

He started as she tapped him on his shoulder. Handing his glass to him silently, she resumed her seat.

'We have to damage control,' he said suddenly.

'What?' she asked. 'How?'

'We can't let the people know that we have stolen a woman from the British camp. We will have to hide her. Camouflage. Keep her incognito.' By now his face was a beetroot red.

'I don't understand,' said Minnie. 'What's in your mind, dear? Tell me.'

A pause. Charles seemed to be thinking hard. A nerve on his left temple twitched. And then: 'If we let her go to the palace the word will spread. And then we will have to face the local anger. Plus the British's wrath will break on our heads. We cannot let her get into the palace. We cannot let the word go around.'

'So, when the maharaja reaches home in a few hours, where do you propose he should go?' Minnie asked, uncomprehending.

'Er ... you know he has been good to us.' He paused and Minnie waited patiently. She sensed what would follow. He continued: 'Let her remain with us. She is white and can pass off as our daughter. And everyone knows that Florence was supposed to visit us this year. So we could always give out that it is Florence who has arrived to be with us.'

'I get your point,' said Minnie weighing the matter. 'And the maharaja ...'

'... would divide his time between the palace and our abode. You know this is a decent enough home, too. Not as luxurious as the palace but comfortable enough for royalty. Until some other arrangement is made, the English woman lives here with us as our daughter, Florence.'

Charles had made the decision after serious deliberation.

'Once the dust settles down we can take appropriate action.' Having arrived at this resolution, Charles looked relieved.

'As you say, dear,' Minnie picked up the tray and went into the kitchen to give instructions for dinner. She had to make arrangements for a house guest. Rather, two house guests.

Charles Bryan had to stop Rajen from entering the royal palace. He mounted his horse and rode out of the palace

gates, passing by the Moti Bagh Gurudwara. It was Gurpurab –
Guru Nanak Dev's birthday celebrations – and there was a
crowd of devout people thronging the courtyard. His horse
galloped through the streets of the city. The sun had set long
ago and the lanes he rode through were dark and deserted.
Dim candles and diyas lit up the windows of the homes he
passed. Electricity had not yet found its way to the royal city.
He rode through the village of Lehal on the outskirts of Patiala.
According to the local belief, a century ago, under a huge
banyan tree here, Guru Tegh Bahadur had taken shelter one
day and blessed the hamlet. Although Bryan was a staunch
Catholic, he had a deep respect for all religions. He bowed
his head in reverence. The Sikhs in particular had been good
to him. In turn he admired their devotion to their faith and
the goodness of their hearts. This particular tree by the side
of a little pond, called Dukhnivaran, was reputed to have
miraculous healing powers. Perhaps one day he would bring
Florence here. She would pray to this tree, sprinkle some of
this magic water on herself, and be cured of her ailments.

He left Lehal behind and rode swiftly towards the
Mughalserai of Rajpura, for that was the route that Rajen
and his horsemen would generally take on the way back from
Simla. He had barely covered ten miles when, near the fort of
Bahadurgarh he heard the sound of approaching hoofs and
realised that it was the maharaja with his posse. Although it was
dark, the moon was bright. The maharaja's men saw the lone
rider waving to them, signalling them to stop. Drawing nearer,
they discovered that it was the trusted Charles Bryan.

'What is it, Charles?' asked Rajen in surprise, drawing
his steed to a halt. 'What are you doing here in the middle
of the night?'

Charles rode close up to him and saw that in the buggy accompanying the maharaja was a frail, tired young girl partly covered with the maharaja's riding cloak. Still on horseback, Charles bowed to her with respect as he spoke to his master.

'Your Highness, I have come to escort you personally,' said Charles. 'There are some precautions to take, some important matters to discuss before you go to your palace.'

'What could be so urgent, Charles, that it can't wait for tomorrow? I have brought you a new maharani. She has to be installed with all due respect.'

'Yes, Your Highness, but first we need to discuss some security issues. You will kindly be my guest for tonight. I pray you, come with me to my lodgings.'

There was a note of urgency in his tone that made Rajen accept the invitation. Looking down at Betty's half-closed eyes, he knew that she was exhausted after the long ride. Perhaps it would be a good idea to let Minnie take care of her tonight.

Rajen and his men followed Charles Bryan back to Patiala. Instead of going to the main palace Rajen and Betty went into Charles and Minnie's apartment.

The long, dusty ride was too much for Betty. She collapsed as soon as she dismounted from the buggy but Minnie was there to support her. She led her to the room she had readied for her, helped her bathe and change into one of her dresses, gave her something to eat and tucked her in bed, clucking soothingly all the time. Almost immediately, Betty fell asleep.

Meanwhile, Rajen and Charles had withdrawn into the study and were engrossed in earnest conversation. Rajen was tired after the strenuous journey but he was impatient to get back to Betty who, he thought, must be waiting for him. Charles fixed him a strong drink – the famous Patiala peg – and held him back, explaining the gravity of the situation, and they discussed the steps they could possibly take, now that it was not possible to undo what had been done. Betty was with him in Patiala and here she would remain. The logistics had to be worked out.

'I know, Charles, when the British government finds out they will not like it. But, come to think of it, why should they object? I may not be a white man but I am a king in my own right. I love her and want her as my queen. She will have all the privileges due to her. Give it time and they will come around,' Rajen was confident.

'And what about the maharani sahiba?' asked Charles.

'Yes, I agree, that is a tough nut to crack. She will be very upset. I will try to handle her with kid gloves. It won't be easy though,' Rajen grinned sheepishly.

Then Charles outlined the plan he had been working on all evening: 'Let the young lady stay in my home for the time being. I will announce that my daughter Florence is visiting me. This will buy us some time and we can plan our strategy. Meanwhile you may come and go as and when you please, just like before.'

It was late and Rajen was too tired to argue, so he agreed. Minnie came in and told him that Betty was fast asleep but he did not wish to leave her there alone; he had to go to her. After all, it was for him that she had left her home and people. Now he was honour-bound to be by her side. He would stay with her tonight and every night. Of that he was sure. Nothing would part them.

By the time he had washed and changed, Betty was in deep sleep. Rajen stood by her bedside watching her. Her face was pale and her breath was slow and even. A lamp by her bedside cast a flickering shadow on her face. Silently he eased himself into an enormous chair by her bedside and sat motionless for a long time. The events of the day had been tumultuous but Rajen was none the worse for it. The day's fatigue had worn off with the cold bath and the stiff drink he had shared with Charles. He felt rejuvenated once more. But he did not wish to disturb Betty. So he simply sat looking at her, waiting for her to wake up.

Sometime in the middle of the night Betty turned in her sleep. She opened her eyes, looked around the unfamiliar room. The taper had burned out but the moonlight filtered in through the long glass windows. She found the maharaja dozing in the armchair. Without the jewel-crested turban on his head he looked unfamiliar. His hair framed his face and hung loose about the nape of his neck. No longer in his shining clothes proclaiming his royal status, he was now clad in a simple tunic with baggy trousers. There was something very vulnerable about him as he lay slumped on the settee, his chest heaving rhythmically, the moonbeams playing softly on his face.

Tiptoeing to his side she touched him on the shoulder and he started.

'Did I frighten Your Majesty?' she was apologetic.

'Oh no, my queen,' he was now wide awake. 'I must have fallen asleep as I sat watching you.'

Immediately wide-awake, he picked up her slender frame and placed her on his lap. She sat like an obedient child, looking into his eyes with trust and confidence.

'You must be tired,' he murmured softly as she nestled against his chest.

'Hm-m-m. Not any more. I feel rested.'

She played with the rings on his finger, fingered the thick gold *kara* on his wrist, traced the outline of the veins on the back of his hand, and drew circles on the thick hair on his forearms. He talked to her gently, caressing her fair hair, tickling the lobe of her ear, running his fingers down her throat, down to the oversized mole in the hollow of her neck. He was not in a hurry. He knew that Betty was now his and he did not wish to frighten her by rushing matters to a head. This was not just another relationship. It was a relationship that was meant to last. So he took his time, talking to her softly, like a gently gurgling rivulet, winning her confidence, as the night wore on.

Betty relaxed in his lap as he kept stroking her hair, face and neck. Then a gentle snore told him she had fallen asleep again. He picked her up slowly and took her back to the four-poster bed. Adjusting the pillows under her head he blew out the candle and lay down beside her.

IN THE MIDST OF ROYALTY

The royal household was quite accustomed to the maharaja's whims and fancies. They had long accepted his pleasure jaunts to Simla, his passion for polo, his horse-riding, his interest in motorcars and whatever else his fancy chose to dwell on. For that matter, so had the masses accepted their ruler in toto. They knew he was a good man, a benevolent maharaja, a good hunter, horse-rider, and above all, a god-fearing leader who loved his people. They knew that every weekend he would go to Simla, hobnobbing with the whites. But that, they reasoned, was part of his job. As the ruler it was his duty to be on good terms with stronger powers that may turn hostile any time.

The next morning was a Sunday and the royal household would together go to pray at the family gurudwara adjacent to the palace. This, being Gurpurab, was a special occasion and Rajen, as the head of the family, had duties to perform. He left Betty, still recovering from fatigue, in Minnie's care and returned to the main palace. Seeking his aged mother, the rajmata, he bowed low and touched her feet. She was counting the beads of her rosary and absent-mindedly blessed him. Then he went to the maharani's suite.

The maharani was in the boudoir, getting dressed for the morning prayers. She wore a yellow salwar-kameez edged with green. A maid was seated by a child's crib in the corner, playing with an infant – the little prince Bhupinder. Another one stood by the queen, combing her lush dark hair, braiding a red *paraanda* into the tresses. On the dressing table lay a casket full of jewellery that the queen would shortly don. Seeing Rajen framed in the doorway, the maharani quickly rose, covered her head with her dupatta and bowed before him, touching his feet. She was a good woman and Rajen respected her. But he also knew that she was possessive and had to be handled with care. She would not agree to the idea of sharing her husband with another woman.

Normally Rajen would take out his motor car whenever they had to go to the gurudwara, although it was barely half a mile away. But not today. He had made up his mind that the next time he would drive his car; it would be with Betty by his side. So they took the royal buggy and went to the gurudwara together, with a little detour of the city. The roads were crowded and people thronged in large numbers to have a glimpse of them: Rajen, the maharani, the little prince and the rajmata. After paying obeisance at the sanctum sanctorum and giving alms to the beggars lined up outside, they walked down the aisle to their waiting buggies and drove back to the palace. Rajen did not go in with the maharani and rajmata. He walked out again, heading for Charles's lodgings. The women saw him leave but did not protest. No questions were asked. No eyebrows were raised. He was the maharaja and free to do as he wished.

Betty was up, bathed and cheerful when he met her at the Bryan's apartment. Minnie had given her a pretty peach dress to wear which highlighted her pink complexion and clear blue eyes. She looked relaxed and very much at home.

The Bryans' lodging comprised a large independent wing of the palace which included two big halls, an antechamber, a huge study, six independent suites, a common dining area, bathing cells, kitchen, pantry and servants' quarters. It was part of the main palace and yet separate from it. Two of the suites with an independent access were now given to Betty. The maharaja, they knew, would be in and out of the premises at will.

It was Betty's first day in Patiala and Rajen wanted her to be happy. She should not regret her decision. He gave instructions to Charles and Betty that she should be provided a fresh wardrobe, jewellery, shoes, accessories, and whatever else her heart should desire. Betty had fled Simla with just the clothes and the little jewellery she wore on her person. But, yes, she had brought with her the large ruby Rajen had pinned on her dress the night before on the terrace of the

Viceregal Lodge. That was his first gift of love. How could she leave it behind?

Betty was reclining on the sofa against the window when Rajen tapped on the door. She sprang up and rushed to him joyfully. He was relieved. All the tension and the apprehensions that had troubled him since morning evaporated with that one smile. It was writ large on her face that she was happy and in love. That she was comfortable with Minnie Bryan clucking around her like a mother hen. Rajen was confident that soon, very soon, matters would settle down and he would be able to present his new maharani to his people. But she had to get used to the Punjabi culture, customs and mannerisms. Minnie could possibly be a go-between and initiate her into the Patiala lifestyle. Then she would be accepted by the people as one of them.

STORM IN THE BRITISH CAMP

As Charles Bryan had feared, all hell broke loose in the British camp. The summer capital was rife with rumours and apprehensions. Long after Betty and Rajen had clattered down the hill on horseback, eyewitnesses stood around the spot where the young English girl had been literally swept off her feet and taken away on the galloping steed. A large crowd gathered, especially when the nannies came out of the church and looked around for their ward. The other two girls in their custody claimed ignorance of what had happened. They were all visibly in a state of shock.

By the evening almost the entire population of Simla was gathered on the Mall – at the point where the upper road leading from the church and ridge towards the Hindu Temple on the other end dips down to touch the Mall. The little hill town was all agog with the news. But who was the girl? And who was the dashing young man sporting a turban? Nobody was quite sure. Besides, where did they go? Perhaps they simply rode off for a ride in the woods and would be back soon. Such escapades were not unheard of. So the nannies and the other two girls who had accompanied Betty waited. In any case, they were hesitant to go back to the Viceregal Lodge with one girl missing. How would they explain it to the lord and the lady? So they continued to wait. Bystanders who had gathered there stood around for a while. At first they conversed in high-pitched excited tones but then, as the day wore on, the excitement too petered off. A few remained hanging out there, the rest went their ways.

By the time the sun started its descent behind the distant range of hills, it was clear that their wait was in vain. Mlle Berton, Betty's governess, and the nanny who was in charge of the other two girls accompanying them to the church from the Viceregal Lodge, decided to turn back and report what had taken place earlier in the day. They were apprehensive, no doubt, but at the same time, something at the back of their mind gave them a false hope – what if she has actually returned home? Perhaps the young horseman simply gave her a ride back home. After all, they did ride away in the same direction. A different road, no doubt, but that road, too led to the Viceregal Lodge, so probably he had taken her home after an adventurous ride in the wooded hills. Hopefully it was just that and nothing more.

Reasoning thus, they reached the Viceregal Lodge in the gathering gloom when the lights were beginning to come on. They inquired at the gate and were told that Betty had not yet reached home. The guests who had attended the party the night before had all gone back. The viceroy had been summoned to Delhi for a meeting with the Secretary of the State for India; his wife was up in her boudoir, resting. An ominous silence enveloped the building where, just the night before, a raucous party had taken place with song, music and dance. As the wheels of their buggies trundled away, the governess and the nanny started walking up to the entrance with the two remaining wards. They could sense the eerie silence of the hills. In the distance they could hear the lone cry of a peewit.

Silently they took the two girls upstairs and tucked them in for the night. Then they went to the viceroy's wife and broke the news. The reaction was predictable. Initial astonishment: where was Betty? No, she wasn't there. Where could she go? Oh, my goodness! As for the turbaned rider, he could be none other than Rajinder Singh of Patiala. The viceroy's wife had noted the attention he showered on her daughter the night before. Not with that maharaja, how could she? He's wild. He's already married. Probably has a child or two. How could she be taken in by him?

Then followed anger against the maharaja: he has broken the laws of hospitality. He was our guest and this is how he has repaid us – by kidnapping our daughter! Outrageous, indeed!

The viceroy's wife raged at first, then wept silently. In the absence of her husband there was little she could do. But instinct told her that the news was not to be made public or there would be hell to pay. After all, they were representatives of Her Majesty, the Queen of England. Any insult or injury to them would mean offence against Her Majesty. Moreover, the public humiliation, the shame, the dishonour that would come in tow … . Good God! She shuddered to think of it. Let her husband, the viceroy, come back and take appropriate action.

Two days later, the viceroy, on his return from the plains, was immediately hustled into his private study and apprised of the situation.

There was no denying it. It was a Scandal. A Scandal with a capital S.

There was no other way the viceroy could describe it. Betty had been abducted. Kidnapped. Captured. But, eyewitnesses said she had gone to him of her own free will. They had seen her running towards the horse, calling out to the rider. What was it then, if not an abduction? An elopement? Good gracious! And that too with a turbaned Indian? It was a scandal, all right.

Rajinder Singh! The maharaja they had trusted so much. How could he do it? How could he go against Her Majesty's regents? Was he not afraid of the repercussions? If the imperial government wished it could take back the honours bestowed on the state of Patiala and crush it in no time. Queen Victoria would arch her eyebrow, look down disdainfully and utter her famous phrase showing disapproval: 'We are not amused!'

This was outrageous, indeed! Her Majesty would certainly not be amused.

The viceroy was at his wits' end. Sheer disbelief at first was followed by uncontrollable rage. Angrily he paced up and down the hall, his hands clenched behind his back, a frown creasing his forehead. His wife sat silently in the corner, twisting the corner of a handkerchief helplessly. The clock on the mantelpiece ticked away loudly – the only sound that could be heard other than the squeaking of the viceroy's boots as he walked up and down the wooden floors.

It was already three days since Betty had disappeared. Without further delay, some action had to take place. The viceroy rang the bell and summoned his first officer. The two then withdrew to a corner of the great hall for an earnest discussion. The first officer was sworn to secrecy before he was apprised of the situation. Something terrible had taken place and a solution had to be found. An elopement between master and slave was unheard of. In this case Betty represented the ruler and Rajinder Singh was nothing but a vassal chief who had to bow down to orders. They would put him in his place. But he had to return Betty to them first. They would deal with him subsequently.

The first officer was given instructions and dispatched to Patiala with a missive. Rajinder Singh, accused of forcible possession of British property (Betty, in this case) was to render an unconditional apology to the British and return the stolen item. No other negotiation was possible. In case he refused to comply there would be dire consequences. He would be proclaimed a public offender and suitable action would be taken against him.

All this was to be conveyed to Rajinder Singh privately. The viceroy did not want the public to know of the event. It would be far too humiliating. So, as far as possible, the exchange would have to take place in secret, without a public hue and cry.

PRECIOUS MOMENTS

Rajen was late that evening. Affairs of the state had kept him busy all day. By the time he came to Betty's chamber it was dark. He entered silently and stood watching her from the doorway. Betty was bent over a desk in one corner of the room, writing something in the light of a candle. The desk was a new addition to the room. It had not been there earlier. Betty had asked Minnie for a table where she could read and write and here it was – a dark mahogany table with carved legs. A sheaf of papers, an open notebook, an inkpot, pens, and some writing material were placed on the table. Two carved chairs were placed by the side, with Betty seated on one. She was bent over a notebook, chewing her pencil thoughtfully. Her hair was tied neatly at the nape of the neck but a few wisps hung loose about her face. A stray curl fell across her forehead and she pushed it out of her eyes as she continued to write.

Rajen stood behind her silently. Turning around, she sprang up happily.

'Oh, at last! I missed you so much. You are late,' she said.

He did not respond. Instead he embraced her fondly and asked: 'What are you doing, my love?'

'Nothing much, my lord. Just putting my thoughts together.'

He picked up the notebook but she took it away from him saying, 'It's nothing, really. I like keeping a diary, so I asked Minnie to give me some writing material.'

'In any case,' she continued, 'I have little to do. Sitting by myself I tend to get bored. So I thought let me write my thoughts down.'

By this time Rajen was seated on the easy chair and she had taken her place on his lap. This was their favourite position together.

'Is there anything in particular you would like to do, my dear?' Rajen asked.

She was silent and seemed to be thinking deeply.

He continued: 'I have made arrangements and from tomorrow you will have two new companions. They will keep you company, work for you and also help you adjust to the palace. And, yes, they know how to speak in English so you will not have much problem communicating with them.'

'Oh, thank you,' she seemed happy as she took his large hands in hers and kissed them gratefully. She did have Minnie's servants take care of her needs but two more just for herself would be a welcome addition.

After a pause, she asked: 'Have you spoken to your mother?'

'No, not yet,' he answered. 'I am waiting for a suitable moment.'

'And the maharani?' she wanted to ask but did not. He would tell her on his own. So she kept silent.

'Well, what do you do all day, my lord?' she asked after a pause.

'Think of you, my sweetheart,' he replied with a smile.

'What besides?' she asked, tracing patterns on his chest.

'Well, let me see. What did I do today? In the morning I approved the building plans of an orphanage in the city. At noon I called a meeting of the commanders of the forces and studied their reports. In the afternoon I laid the foundation of a new hospital. It will be called Rajindra Hospital, bigger than the Lady Dufferin Hospital that we now have. And then I went to the polo grounds, followed by half an hour at billiards. And ... I think that's it. And now, at night, I have come to my darling,' Rajen stroked her hair gently as he talked. 'As you can see, it is a busy life.'

'So many duties,' she responded sleepily.

'And as you know, my duties are not over,' he smiled into her face. 'Nor yours, my dear. We still have a lot to do.'

'Hm-mmm, yes,' Betty smiled happily.

She buried her face in his shoulder as he continued to stroke her hair.

The emissary from the viceroy came a few days after Betty was installed at the Bryans. He had a meeting with the maharaja *in camera* and conveyed the message of the viceroy. Return the girl and he would be forgiven. Or else, face the wrath of the British monarch. This message was conveyed in the privacy of the maharaja's chamber. It was essential that the news of the elopement should not be leaked out to the public.

The messenger explained to the maharaja how grave the consequences of his action could be. Unless he took corrective steps immediately there would be a major disturbance in the balance of power in the country. As the rulers of the Indian subcontinent, the British could not, in any circumstances, allow one of their subjugated petty vassal kings to abduct the daughter of the senior-most official of the British Empire. It would be best for the maharaja to go back over what he had done and make amends.

But Rajen was unfazed. Abduction? What abduction? He was adamant that it was not abduction, and that Betty had come with him of her own free will. So, what's so strange about that? – he wanted to know. His method may have been unusual but his intentions were honourable. He wanted to marry the viceroy's daughter and make her his queen. Was it dishonourable to wish to marry? Rajen sent back the messenger with this message for the viceroy.

Betty had been in Patiala for just a few days but she was getting used to the ways of the palace. She did not miss her life in Simla nor her past as the viceroy's daughter, for there were so many new things around her, so much of novelty that she was being introduced to. Rajen was good to her. So were Charles and Minnie. Thanks to them, she now had a new wardrobe and whatever else she could wish for. Minnie would spend time with her, telling her about the state, its robust and hard-working people, its customs and traditions. She and Charles had spent just a couple of years in Patiala but it had grown on them and they were now quite at home in these surroundings.

Charles and Minnie had given out that their daughter, Florence was finally in Patiala, visiting them. It was accepted without a murmur. The maharaja's increased number of visits to their apartments did not raise any eyebrows, either. He used to come and go frequently earlier, too. So the fact that now it was for Betty that he visited the Bryans went unnoticed. At least for some time.

Betty would spend the day by herself, sometimes in the company of Minnie Bryan and sometimes bending over her notebook on the desk. She filled page after page with her large spidery handwriting, ornate with loops and curls and flourishes. When she was not working at it, the notebook was kept locked in the drawer of the desk and the key hidden safely in some secret place.

The two new companions were vivacious young girls called Jasbir and Harbir. They were daughters of the maharaja's commander-in-chief who was well-versed in English and had made it a point to teach his children the imperial language, well aware of the advantages that would come with a proficiency in English. Betty, however, was more interested in learning Punjabi from her companions. Every day she would spend a couple of hours learning the Punjabi alphabet. She would try conversing with them in the local language. She tried to learn their folk songs and even their dances. She asked questions about the history of the royal state, about their religion, about their gurus and gurudwaras. Jasbir and Harbir were delighted with the progress of their pupil and put their heart and soul into their job. Every day they would teach her something new amid much mirth and laughter.

One day Betty, while conversing with her companions, mentioned that she would like to try out a Punjabi outfit. The two girls almost jumped with glee, so excited were they at the thought of dressing up Betty as a Punjabi *kudi*. But, insisted Betty, it had to be in secret. She wanted to surprise the maharaja. Agreeing readily, the companions set about plotting and planning. Jasbir was about the same size as Betty, so perhaps she could try out one of her salwar-suits. And Harbir's foot size was the same as Betty's, so she could borrow her *juttis*. Betty tried out their clothes. At first they felt strange. Not at all like the long dresses and skirts she was accustomed to wearing. But after a couple of trials she realised how comfortable she felt in the Punjabi dress.

In the evening the companions would go back home and Betty would prepare to receive the maharaja. He would come without fail. Sometimes he was late but he never missed out on Betty. Once in a while they would share a drink with the Bryans. Charles and Rajen would have their Patiala peg while Minnie and Betty (who was now called Florence) would settle for gin and tonic. Later, Charles and Minnie would retire to their own rooms and leave Betty and Rajen alone.

Rajen told Betty about the visit of the viceroy's messenger and the reply he had sent back. She listened carefully without reacting.

'I told him I wish to marry you and make you my queen. That is not a crime, is it?' he asked.

She smiled: 'When?'

He knew that she wanted an answer. 'I am working on it, trust me, Betty,' he said.

In his mind he had worked out all the pros and cons. The upside as well as the downside of the matter.

SETTING THE HOUSE IN ORDER

Actually there was little upside to it. It was all downside. In the first place, what he wanted was an alliance between two political powers and the powers were unequal. Although he was a king in his own right, he could not overlook the fact that his kingdom was subservient to the British and he could ill-afford to vex them. This was the major problem. The *goras* would not be happy about it. Nor would his own people. How could the ruler of a proud city-state choose a *gori* woman for his consort?

But, as he reasoned with himself, the heart had its reasons that may not be denied. The heart would find a way.

The other problems were not so great, or so he reckoned. The maharani, his wife, would sulk but may not pose much of a problem, knowing full well that as the king it was his prerogative to have multiple wives if he so wished. However, he knew that there may be resistance from her paternal family. A proud and self-respecting community that saw itself as the foremost warrior class in the Punjab, they would probably be averse to the idea of a girl from their community being supplanted by another.

Rajen went looking for his mother, the rajmata. She was not in the prayer room. Nor was she in the *baithak*. Finally he found her in her boudoir. She was reclining on a divan, examining some jewels which were displayed before her in a tray covered with a navy-blue velvet cloth. As she fingered the precious stones embedded in ornate gold work, she picked out a few items and placed them aside. She was making preparations for her daughter's visit to the palace. Rajen's sister, Bibi Bachtiar, who was married to the magistrate of Lahore, was to visit Patiala the following week with her children and husband. Appropriate gifts and jewellery had to be given to them and the rajmata was busy with her selection.

Seeing Rajen enter the room, she asked him to help her make a selection. Rajen had other matters perturbing him but he respectfully obliged, taking his seat on a low stool at his mother's feet. As she examined one glittering ornament after another, she passed it on to her son for his comments. He looked at them disinterestedly, made a few appropriate remarks now and then. Finally, the selection was done, the jewels were put away, and the rajmata leaned back against the bolster, eyeing her son keenly. She could see there was something important on his mind. Dismissing the maids who hovered around her, she turned to him.

'What is it, *puttar*?'

Rajmata was beautiful, even at this age. Her face was unlined and smooth. Her hands were soft and pink. Her complexion was a healthy wheatish. Her hair, under the embroidered dupatta on her head, was salt and pepper. She was dressed in an off-white silk salwar-kameez. Around her neck was a heavy gold chain on which hung a *khanda*. On her right wrist she sported a thick gold bangle. This was all the jewellery that the queen mother wore. She had been widowed almost two decades ago and since then she had lived a low-profile life in the palace. However, she remained abreast of whatever transpired in the corridors of power. She was also reasonably well-informed of what went on in the private chambers of the palace. She knew for a fact that her son was spending little time with his wife and infant. She also knew that his visits to the Bryans had become more frequent and that they had a young and beautiful daughter visiting them currently who was the object of the maharaja's attention.

But she was his mother. She understood him and she forgave him even before he asked for sympathy and support. And now, finding him distracted, she reached out for his hand, held it gently and repeated her question.

'What is it, *puttar*?'

He was silent. He did not know where to begin. She was a shrewd mother and could guess what was on his mind.

'You want to talk about Miss Bryan, don't you?' she came directly to the point.

Miss Bryan. The name was unfamiliar to Rajen and he realised with a start that she was referring to Betty. After all, in Patiala she was known as the Bryans' daughter, Florence. Let it remain so, thought Rajen.

'Yes,' he replied and remained silent.

She read his thoughts.

'You wish to marry her?' it was more of a statement than a question.

'Yes, mother,' he was relieved that she had made it easy for him.

She took a deep breath and closed her eyes.

'*Puttar*, she is not from our *kaum* or *dharma*. Our people would not accept her easily.'

He remained silent, his head respectfully bowed.

She continued: 'But let me think about it. We will find a way out.'

'But, mother,' he began and then hesitated. Should he, or should he not apprise her of the reality? That she was the viceroy's daughter and not the Bryans'?

'What is it, *puttar*? There's something else, isn't it?'

Something held him back. He could not bring himself to tell her that he had come away with the viceroy's daughter. The queen mother would be outraged.

Seeing that he did not wish to communicate, the elderly woman sighed and dropped the matter. In her heart of hearts she hoped that her son would soon tire of his latest interest. A young man's heart is wild and gets attracted to novelty. Rajen, she knew, had a weakness for petite English girls with fair skin and light hair. But, hopefully, it would soon pass. Give him time, she thought to herself, and he will turn his passion in another direction, to something else.

For the time being, she told her son that they would think of a strategy and sent him away.

On his part, Rajen felt relieved. It was a load off his head. He had confided in his mother and she had taken it in her stride. True, he had not yet told her the truth about Betty's identity but let her first get used to the idea of having a *gori* daughter-in-law, then he would enlighten her. Meanwhile, perhaps the viceroy would come around, too, and the matter would be less complicated.

It was late evening and Rajen, tired after a stimulating game of polo on the Baradari grounds, headed for the palace. He would bathe and change in his chambers and then go to Betty. Just the thought of her made him smile. He was glad that she had adjusted to her new life in the palace. She seemed happy and cheerful. Moreover, she was showing a keen interest in the culture of the royal city, the music, art and craft. This was a good sign. As the future maharani she needed to be well-informed.

When he knocked at Betty's door he was surprised to find it ajar. He called out to her but there was no response. He went into the inner room and paused at the doorway in surprise. In the middle of the room stood an unfamiliar woman with her face covered. She wore a red and gold salwar-kameez with her head and face covered with a phulkari dupatta. Below the dupatta a long multicolored *paraanda* was slung over her shoulder.

As Rajen gaped in surprise, the girl, her face still covered, joined her palms respectfully, bowed her head, and said, *'Sat siri akal!'*

He heard the voice and chuckled. It was Betty.

'Betty! What's all this?' he asked and drew her close. Lifting her veil he uncovered her head. Her hair was braided back in the Punjabi fashion. There were red glass bangles on her wrists and her feet were shod in gold *juttis*. This was the first time he had seen her dressed like a local Punjabi girl and she looked stunning.

There was more in store for the maharaja. Betty broke free, spread her dupatta with both arms like a pair of wings and broke into a song, her body moving rhythmically from side to side as she sang: *'Jei mahiya mainu nachdi vekhna, ucha mehal pawa dei ...'*

In all probability she did not know the meaning of the song. It was just something she had learnt from her companions and memorised it for the pleasure of the maharaja. The dance was an attempt at *giddha*, popular among the women of Punjab. Betty sang with a strong English accent and twirled about the room, her hips swaying, her arms slicing the air in graceful, feminine moves.

Rajen was pleased. He liked her spirit. She was young, she was vivacious, and she was captivating, indeed. She had something new for him every day. He loved her for it.

The viceroy's messenger came to Patiala a second time. Once again the visit was shrouded in secrecy. Once again there was a closed-chamber serious talk with the maharaja. And once again the maharaja sent the messenger back, assuring him that Betty was being well taken care of and that he had no intention of sending her back. On hearing this, the messenger informed the maharaja of the viceroy's decision to apprise the English Crown of the matter. In the meantime Maharaja Rajinder Singh's name would be blacklisted and he would be barred entry into Simla. He was warned of further disciplinary action if he refused to cooperate. But Rajinder Singh simply smiled, looked unruffled, and said he would face the repercussions. Just before he left, the messenger asked if he could meet Betty personally.

'Why not?' replied the maharaja. You may see her tonight at our lodgings. Join us for an exclusive dinner.

The maharaja gave instructions that the Bryans should make arrangements for hosting a dinner for the viceroy's emissary. Betty would receive him personally.

The dinner was a quiet affair. Betty, formally dressed in a deep maroon evening gown, a cashmere stole thrown across her shoulders, dignified and sombre in her demeanour, received the guest in the main parlour of the Bryan's apartment and they sat for dinner at the table, waited upon by a retinue of attendants. The Bryans joined them at the table. Drinks were served and the meal was lavish, all in the true Patiala style. Some conversation took place but it was guarded and avoided all controversial matters.

Then suddenly the maharaja, who had seemed preoccupied so far, made an announcement that surprised the others on the table.

'In the coming summer, I will invite you to my palace in Himachal. Not far from Simla, but a hundred metres higher in altitude. Tell the viceroy I would be happy to receive him once the winter is over and the plains warm up again.'

This was news. The messenger, the Bryans, and Betty looked at him in surprise as he continued:

'I do not need to visit Simla again because I am making my own palace for my dear wife, the chhoti maharani of Patiala,' and he raised his hand to his lips, blowing a kiss in Betty's direction, even as they looked on in surprise.

They were not yet married but Rajen had called her wife and maharani. Betty, flushed, sat demurely looking down at her hands clasped in her lap.

'It will have the highest cricket pitch in the world,' he continued. 'Tell His Excellency, the viceroy, that I would like to invite his eleven to come and play with my team any time after Easter.'

The messenger replied, cautiously, 'I will certainly convey it to His Lordship. And whereabouts would your palace be located, Sir?'

'Not far from Simla, and yet as scenic. As beautiful if not more. Construction will be over sooner than you know.'

This was his way of retaliating to the viceroy's message debarring him from entering Simla. An alternative hill resort was an idea he had been toying with ever since he and Betty fled from Simla. The half-formed thought was thus suddenly given its formal, concrete shape on the spur of the moment. Let the Englishmen keep Simla for themselves, he reasoned. He would have a better, more beautiful haven for himself and Betty. His very own Mount Olympus, an ethereal vantage point much higher than the English summer capital. More beautiful and more scenic, closer to the high heavens, with a splendid palace atop the hill that would outshine any resort constructed by the Englishmen.

Thus was born the idea of Chail Palace. An idea that would soon fructify into reality. An Olympus higher than the summer capital of the *angrez-log*.

The summer capital of the British rulers, meanwhile, was beginning to wear a deserted look as the year drew to a close.

The last of the loaded wagons trundled out of the Simla hills, slowly and painstakingly avoiding all the jagged corners of the mountainside. The long caravan of horse-riders, horse-carts and bullock-driven covered wagons wound its way down to the plains, carrying with them the ruling white population of the country. Officers and subordinates. Wives and mothers and children. Official correspondence, stationery, household goods, foodstuff, books, toys, and other paraphernalia necessary for a normal day-to-day existence. With the onset of every winter long convoys transporting the ruling class and its families would embark on the 1200-mile long journey from Simla to Calcutta. The convoy comprised assorted modes of transport – barges, elephants, camels, horses, bullock carts – all of them moving slowly but steadily down the hill, over the plains, across rivers and fords, towards the east, towards the winter capital of the British Raj.

The local population of Simla was used to this phenomenon. Year after year, in the month of April, the long line of horses and carts would labour up the winding mountainous roads, bringing with them the white population – men, women and children with delicate constitutions unable to bear the heat of the plains. Year after year, in early November, before the first snowfall, before the mountains became too cold and inhospitable for a comfortable living, the same exodus would take place from the hills into the plains. The locals were used to it. Yet they lined up along the roadside to watch them go by, emptying the little hill town of its fun and frolic, taking with them the mirth and gaiety, the parties and picnics, the theatre and the entire summer culture of Simla. It was a fascinating sight every time the seasons changed. Rickshaw coolies and tonga drivers would watch stone-faced, knowing that their earnings would dwindle to a zero with the departure of the *sahib-log*. Others who stayed behind – the locals – would silently watch from rooftops, from windows and the upper reaches of the hills.

A veil of silence would settle on the hill-top with the fall of the temperature. People left behind would huddle indoors against the approaching cold. With the turn of the year, a blanket of snow would cover all the hills. Life would seem to drift into a slumber, hibernating patiently, waiting for the onset of spring once more.

The viceroy and his wife, in one of the carriages trundling downhill on the zigzag bumpy road, were in a sombre mood. They had come to the summer capital with their daughter and were going back without her now. Initially it was anger that raged in them. The ruling class, they were convinced, should remain with its ilk. Birds of a feather should flock together. A daughter from their household had no business to run away with a native. They had lost Betty to the ruler of a vassal state. Why did she do this to them? From the reports of the messenger they had sent it appeared as though Betty was well-adjusted but they were not satisfied. Gradually, however, the anger subsided. Instead there was now anxiety. What was the way out? How would they explain it to Her Majesty, Queen Victoria? What action would they take? The viceregal couple was in a quandary. They had plenty of time to rue over the matter and contemplate appropriate further action as the journey to Calcutta was long and dusty. It had to be accomplished with frequent stops and starts.

HARNAM KAUR

A NEW LIFE

Florence Bryan, as Betty was known in Patiala, had been at the palace for three months. In these three months she had made herself at home, befriended a few women and won their hearts. Thanks to Harbir and Jasbir, her companions, she could now speak a few sentences in broken Punjabi. She was now learning how to cook *saag* and *makke di roti*. She had developed a strong taste for the Punjabi style of cooking mutton chops and would invariably prepare some in the evenings, before the maharaja arrived. They would sit together on the loveseat by the window with their drinks, nibbling at the snacks.

Today, however, Betty was feeling tired. She finished preparing the snacks in the kitchen and returned to her room to rest awhile and freshen up before the maharaja's arrival. Barely had she reached the door when her eyes clouded over and the world seemed to turn around. She grabbed a chair for support and sank into it. Minnie ran to her side in panic, led her to the couch and made her lie down.

'What is it, my child?' she asked.

Betty smiled: 'Nothing. I am simply tired.' She shut her eyes.

'You rest here, my dear. Put your feet up. Let me get you a glass of milk.' Minnie fussed around like the mother hen. 'Should I call the doctor?'

'Oh, no, I shall be fine,' Betty assured her.

After a while, when she felt better, she went to her suite. She looked at her face in the mirror. The skin was pale and bloodless. There were faint blotches under her eyes. She was looking weak. But Betty was not worried. She knew the reason. She knew why she had felt faint in the kitchen.

She also knew that the time had come to tell Rajen that marriage could not be postponed for much longer. She would tell the maharaja the good news tonight. Betty was excited at the thought of becoming the mother of a little prince.

So was the maharaja when she broke the news to him later in the evening.

The door was unlatched and he walked in at the usual time. She was sitting by the fireside, busy with a pair of knitting needles. In her lap lay a ball of red wool. When she saw the maharaja enter she put her knitting aside and came to him quickly. He saw the excitement in her eyes, her quirky breath and the tremble in her hands. What surprise did she have in store for him today? He wondered but did not say anything. Holding her hand lightly, he led her to the sofa and sat beside her. She did not climb on to his lap, the way she usually did. Instead she sat facing him, looking intently into his face, as though she were keeping some secret to herself.

'What is it, my little mouse?' he asked.

'Nothing,' she said as she picked up her knitting needles again. The needles went click-click as she looped the yarn over her finger, moving it in and out, back and forth.

'What are you knitting?' he asked.

She kept silent. A smile played on her face as the needles kept clicking steadily.

And then she paused. Altogether she had knitted about four inches in stocking stitch. Placing her handiwork on her lap, she folded it double and tried it on her wrist like a little cap.

'How does it look?'

'What?' he asked, 'it looks like a cap.'

'It is,' she replied.

'And whose cap is it, my little mouse?' he tweaked her nose.

'Rajkumar's.'

'Rajkumar? Which rajkumar?'

'My rajkumar,' she said. 'Yours and mine. He's coming soon. On his way. I am getting him ready for you, your lordship.' She got up and stood before him, holding both his hands in hers, placing them flat on her belly.

Rajen stood up, facing her. He looked deep into her eyes and saw the hope and promise in their depths. He saw the eagerness, the excitement veiled beneath a calm demeanour.

He was not new to fatherhood. The badi maharani – as he now thought of his queen, Jasmer Kaur – had given him a son the year before. The toddler, who was the apple of his mother's eye, was the firstborn son of the ruler, and so the crown prince. But, the thought struck the maharaja with some guilt; he had not paid him much attention lately. In fact he had not seen him at all in the last few weeks. The last time he had gone to the badi maharani's chambers he had found her rather withdrawn. She had indirectly questioned him about his visits to the Bryans' place, hinting that she had heard some rumours. The maharaja had been honest with her and confirmed his interest in 'Bryan's daughter' as she was known. With that, the badi maharani had lapsed into silence. The maharaja could sense the chasm yawning between them. A chasm that would not be bridged. That would only become wider.

That particular day, walking out of the badi maharani's apartment, he had a feeling that a chapter was over; a new chapter was to begin now and this time with Betty. He had mixed feelings about it. He was sad for his first wife. But he had been good to her and he would continue taking good care of her. He would see that she was well looked after with all means supporting her. As for the child, the little prince she had given birth to, he would grow up in his own right. The law of the land would be followed and nobody would deny him that.

With the badi maharani, his relationship had always been formal and restrained. Theirs had been an arranged marriage, fixed when they were both far too young to take a decision for themselves. The elders of two royal families had put their heads together and struck a matrimonial alliance between two princely states, Nabha and Patiala. It was the norm, accepted by all concerned, including the bridal couple, still in their early teens.

With Betty, however, his relationship was different. He felt it was more human: there was passion here which was missing in his marriage with the badi maharani. There was love – the kind he had not experienced ever before. There was a longing, a yearning in him whenever he was away from Betty. She had become a part of him, seeping into his very being, a part of his pulse, in the blood of his veins, in the palpitation of his heart and in his waking dreams.

Looking down at Betty now, he suddenly realised how much she meant to him and how much closer they would get once their child completed the picture. He was grateful for the trust he saw in her eyes, for her unquestioning, complete surrender to the circumstances, for the faith she had reposed in him. He would not let her down, of that he was sure. He would never let her regret her decision to sacrifice the world she had grown up in just for his sake.

Rajen seated her on his knee and comforted her. Not that she needed any comforting. She was relaxed now that she had shared her secret with him. As for Rajen, he was aware of an obligation to be fulfilled. A child must have a legitimate father. He would have to arrange for marriage celebrations without further delay. Betty would be his lawfully wedded wife so that the little prince would be born into his rightful place. The palace would be his legal home.

The people of Patiala had accepted Betty unquestioningly as Florence, the Bryans' daughter. After all, there was no reason to suspect that Charles and Minnie were hosting someone other than their own family. True, immediately following the maharaja's return from Simla there were some vague rumours doing the rounds but they were not substantiated and had fizzled out within a few days. Instead, hushed whispers now went around on the real reason behind the maharaja's regular nocturnal visits to the Bryans' apartment. Although nothing was discussed publicly, all eyes and ears were attentive and eagerly waited for further developments. Either the maharaja would tire of his new interest, stop visiting the Bryans, and turn his attention to something else, or he would take the matter seriously and announce a betrothal. Seeing the fresh, innocent beauty of the white girl, the odds were in favour of the latter possibility.

The speculation found its way to the queen mother who summoned her son one morning for breakfast. The maharaja dutifully showed up at his mother's boudoir. In any case, he was planning to meet her that day. Had she not called him he would have sought her out. Over a typically Punjabi breakfast of stuffed *aloo-ke-paranthey*, with lumps of fresh butter and *lassi*, served in silver trays by royal handmaids, the maharaja and his mother talked about the biting cold and the persistent fog. Lohri celebrations, just a week away, would be followed by Basant the harbinger of spring. But for now it was bitterly cold. A roaring fireplace in the corner of the room kept them warm as they talked. Breakfast over, the rajmata dismissed her maids and turned to her son with a serious look on her face.

'Rajen, *puttar*,' she began, eyeing him keenly, 'are you going to marry the Bryans' daughter?'

'Yes, *beeji*,' he avoided looking at her directly, 'I am going to marry Betty.'

'Betty? I was told her name is Florence,' she looked puzzled.

'*Beeji*, that is what I wish to talk to you about. She is not Bryan's daughter, Florence. She is Beatrix...'

'And who is Beatrix?' asked the matriarch, one eyebrow arched questioningly.

A pause. And then, 'Beatrix is the viceroy's daughter.'

Silence. The queen mother's face was expressionless.

Rajen continued in a single breath: 'She is the viceroy's daughter. I brought her to Patiala without the consent of her parents and I wish to marry her. And, beeji, she is going to have my child very soon.'

There. He had said it. The words had just poured out. Words that he had hesitated to utter all this while. The rajmata sat in stony silence, weighing the words. Then she closed her eyes and drew a deep breath.

'*Wahe Guru!*' she exclaimed. 'Tell me all about it. From the beginning.'

Rajen chose his words carefully and in barest outlines told her how he had met Betty at Simla and decided to bring her home as his queen. He had not asked her parents for permission, knowing they would never agree. But, he assured his mother, the girl was willing and he loved her very much.

'Why don't you meet her, *beeji*? You will like her. You will accept her as your daughter-in-law,' it was almost a plea.

She saw the earnest look in his eyes and relented: 'All right, *puttar*, I will meet her. But there are important issues to take care of. I am sure you know that.'

'Yes, *beeji*.' And they entered a long and serious discussion of the likely repercussions of the marriage.

The problems they anticipated were from two main sources. One, the British, the other from within the royal family.

'Let's take the first problem first,' the rajmata had regained her composure by now. 'What do the angrez have to say on the matter?'

'They want her back. That was the last I heard from them. No news, no messenger for the last two months. The capital has moved back to Calcutta. I suppose when they return to Simla in April we can expect further developments.'

The ageing mother sighed, 'Yes. I should think so. We will have to wait and see. But what about the other major problem? If we accept Beatrix as the chhoti maharani, how will the badi maharani take it? How will her brothers react?'

Rajen understood what his mother was driving at. Jasmer Kaur, the badi maharani who had been neglected for the past three months, would not be appeased. She would feel threatened, being replaced by an outsider. Besides, as the mother of Rajen's firstborn, the future maharaja of Patiala, Prince Bhupinder Singh, she was bound to safeguard the interest of her son lest someone else should pull the rug under their feet.

The badi maharani was not likely to do anything by herself but she came from a family of hot-blooded Sikh warriors. Her brothers would probably not accept the idea of their sister being marginalised in the royal house. What reaction would their resentment take? It was hard to say. It could be anything – from a cold-blooded murder to a kidnapping or some other form of violence. Honour killings were not unknown. For the honour of their sister it was not unthinkable that they would ruthlessly obliterate all irritants.

These were the two main hurdles to the maharaja's betrothal to Betty. There was another risk, too. The die-hard Sikhs of Patiala were conservative in matters of religion. Would they accept a queen from another faith?

The rajmata discussed matters with the maharaja seriously in muted tones through the morning. She assured her son that she would meet Beatrix soon. Then, Rajen took leave, bowed before her respectfully to touch her feet, and left for

Qila Mubarak. He had urgent meetings pending. The city of Patiala needed to be spruced up for the coming festive season and he had to make a quick survey of the work being done.

LIVING ON THE FRINGES

The news trickled into the chambers of the badi maharani as she sat in front of the dressing table, getting her long and lustrous hair oiled by her handmaid. The little prince, Yuvraj Bhupinder Singh, was crawling about at her feet. The woman massaging the royal head was skilled at her job. Under her nimble fingers the maharani could feel her scalp warm up. She shut her eyes as she leaned back and relaxed.

The masseuse, Bibi Kulwinder, was an old hand at the palace. She was the maharani's trusted servant and confidante, at her service ever since she had entered the palace some years ago as a young bride. Today, while massaging oil into the royal tresses, she cleared her throat and began talking to her highness.

'Maharani sahiba, will you allow me to speak?'

'Yes, certainly, bibi. What is it?' the maharani replied, her eyes still closed.

Kulwinder was silent for a while, apparently in deep thought. The maharani half-opened an eye and saw the worry-lines on her forehead. She waited for her to speak. Finally, the maid heaved a long sigh and began talking.

She started with a long-winded preamble, reminding the queen of her loyalty and how she had been in the service of the palace ever since she could remember, how her mother and her father and grandfather before them had all been loyal servants of the maharaja. She reminded the queen that she would never do anything wrong, or anything that would harm the interest of the royal family. She swore by all that she considered sacred – Baba Nanak's picture hanging on the wall, the sacred *kara* she wore on her right hand, the Guru Granth Sahib, the Golden Temple, her family, her children, and whatever else she could think of.

The maharani waited patiently for the monologue to end. When would the woman come to the point? – she wondered but heard her out quietly. When the deluge of words did not seem to stop, she gently interrupted: 'Tell me, bibi, what is bothering you.'

Kulwinder stopped massaging the maharani's hair. She fell at her feet and bowing her head, said, 'Punish me if I am wrong. But hear me out and forgive me. You are my *mai-baap* and I have to tell you what is going on.'

She told the maharani about the maharaja's nocturnal visits to the Bryans'. She told her about the Bryans' daughter and the apartment she shared with the maharaja. And finally she told her about rumours she had heard of the maharaja's impending second marriage.

The maharani heard her out in silence. She did not disclose the fact that she had got wind of it earlier. When her royal spouse had stopped visiting her chambers she had wondered why. Some clever investigation by trusted servants had brought back the news to her. She had received it stoically, hoping that the maharaja's new-found affection would be short-lived. He would tire of it and come back to her. But this did not happen. And now there was little chance of him coming back to her. She sighed sorrowfully. The day she was betrothed to the royal family her mother had warned her that women in the royal household had a precarious position. They could expect to be part of a zenana, a harem in which there would be other women for the pleasure of the male members of the royal family. The maharaja had the right to take on more than one wife and she, even if she was his lawfully wedded first wife, could do little to prevent it from happening. She was aware of the possibility but even so, she was disturbed about it. Initially she had had confidence in her self – that she would be able to hold her husband's attention and not let it stray. Alas, within a few months of marriage, she had realised it was impossible.

As Bibi Kulwinder prattled on, a plan was beginning to take shape in the queen's mind. She would not reveal it to anyone but those closest to her, those who would be able to implement it and keep their lips sealed. It had been there at the back of her mind all along, a vague idea of the steps to follow in case of such an eventuality. Now it was time to act and she started giving it a serious thought.

But first, she had to be sure of the facts. She asked Bibi Kulwinder specific questions. Did the maharaja take her out with him in his car? Yes, bibi had seen them driving through the Baradari Gardens one day. The Bryans, Charles and Minnie, were with them. The maharaja was driving the car with the young girl by his side while the Bryans sat in the back seat. Was the girl beautiful? Yes, she was striking to look at – a healthy pink complexion, fair hair, tall and graceful. She was dressed in a cream-coloured long dress, with a bonnet on her head. As the car cruised along slowly, people had gathered by the roadside to wave and cheer. The girl had waved back at them from the car. She seemed happy seated by the maharaja's side.

Has the rajmata met the girl? Kulwinder did not know. But she had information that the maharaja was closeted with his mother for several hours the previous morning and they seemed to discuss something of great importance. Perhaps he had taken his mother into confidence.

Kulwinder was now massaging the maharani's feet with warm scented oil. She continued talking to her in a low monotone, reminding her of her services rendered so far and her devotion to her family. The session over, she gathered up the oils, the towels and the basins. As she turned to the little prince who also needed a massage, the younger maids prepared the water for the bath and laid out the maharani's clothes for the day.

The maharani bathed and dressed. She sat looking at herself in the mirror, wondering how she could make herself appealing to the maharaja again. The mirror faithfully reflected her face – young, beautiful, and intelligent in appearance. What had gone wrong and where? She wondered. She sent a message to the rajmata, asking for an audience. The rajmata responded immediately, telling her to come and see her right away. The maharani, gathering the little prince in her arms, went to the boudoir of the ageing matriarch.

Formal greetings over, she handed the baby to his grandmother who placed him on her lap and started tickling him under the chin as his mother looked on. The maids had been sent away and they had the chamber to themselves when the younger woman said suddenly, 'I wish to go and visit my parents.'

The queen mother looked up and calmly responded with a smile, 'Why not, my dear? We can make arrangements. You can go and meet them over Baisakhi.'

'*Beeji*, Baisakhi is too far. I would like to go sooner. How about next week? Lohri?'

'Lohri? No, *puttar*, it is our *kaka's* first Lohri. I cannot allow my grandchild to be away from the palace on this special occasion. There will be elaborate celebrations. After all, he is the crown prince. But I will make arrangements and you may leave soon after the Lohri celebrations.'

The maharani bowed her head in silence. The rajmata's wishes could not be denied. So be it.

When the badi maharani left, the rajmata did some deep thinking and decided to meet Betty only after Lohri. She had a sense of fairness towards her elder daughter-in-law. Lohri was being celebrated for the firstborn of the next generation, the crown prince. The event should not be diluted with an act that went counter to the spirit of the occasion. So thinking, she sent a message to her son, the maharaja. She would meet the Bryans – and Betty – later in the week, perhaps.

Back in her chambers, the maharani sat at the window, looking out at the grounds below. There was a lively game of polo underway. Through the veil of dust raised by the horses she could distinguish the maharaja's form on his Irish stud. He was clearly the centre of everyone's attention. The game seemed to revolve around him. He rode fast, controlled his horse with practiced skill, and from time to time emitted an excited shout when the game seemed to be going his way. The maharani did not understand much of the game but the excitement was carried across to her.

All this while, as she looked on, she realised how much she missed the maharaja. He looked so young and dashing on his horse. With each move, each stroke, each gesture, he radiated energy. She watched from her balcony until the dusk settled in and the horse-riders brought their game to a close. The maid came to ask if she should serve her dinner but the maharani said she was not hungry and would not eat. Attending to the prince, feeding him and tucking him up in bed, the maid left for the night. The maharani was still sitting at the window, staring vacantly into the dark night. The half-formed idea she had been toying with lately was now taking concrete shape in her mind. She would have to talk to her brothers about it. They would help her.

CELEBRATIONS

Lohri was in the air and Betty, too, was caught up in the excitement.

'What is this Lohri?' she asked her companions, Jasbir and Harbir, when she first heard of the festival.

'We have lots of fun,' they told her. 'We light a big fire, sing, dance, have dry fruit, sweets and *rewri-gajjak.*' They explained what *gajjak* and *rewri* meant, bringing some for her to taste. Betty found them sweet and sticky, different from the sweets she was used to. She preferred the roasted peanuts.

'But why do you celebrate Lohri?' she wanted to know.

The two vivacious girls, eager to educate the English woman, enthusiastically told her what they knew.

Jasbir spoke first: 'Lohri, is celebrated every year on 13 January. It is a festival to worship fire. The first Lohri is very important for newly married couples and for newborn babies. Madam-ji, won't we celebrate your Lohri this time?'

Before Betty could get over her confusion, Harbir interrupted: 'Don't be silly. Madam's Lohri will be next year.

We will celebrate a double Lohri. Madam-ji, won't you give us a *kaka* by then?'

'Shut up,' her sister scolded her. 'You are making her uncomfortable. Madam-ji, on Lohri night people gather around the bonfire and throw *til, gur* and puffed rice into the bonfire. Prayers are offered to the bonfire seeking health and happiness. We dance and sing traditional folk songs like "*sundar mundri ho*".'

She got up and danced a jig as she broke into a lively song.

Harbir continued: 'The entire family gets together over the bonfire. Our maharaja's bonfire is the biggest and grandest bonfire in Patiala. We exchange gifts and we have *sarson ka saag* and *makke ki roti*. We pray for a good harvest.'

'Actually, it celebrates the end of winter and the onset of spring. Lohri is supposed to be the coldest day of the year. After this day the temperature starts rising. You may also call it the beginning of a new year,' Jasbir finished.

And then it was Lohri. There were celebrations galore everywhere. The entire city was decorated with flowers and lit up with lamps. In the inner courtyard of Moti Bagh Palace preparations were made for a huge bonfire. Immense logs of wood were stacked in a pile at the centre. Chairs were placed around it for the royal family and the officers of the palace. There were huge silver containers full of peanuts, puffed rice, *gajjak* and *rewris*. All day long one could hear drumbeats echoing through the city. Groups of young children went from door to door, asking for Lohri sweets.

The rajmata had a lot of work to do. This being her grandson's first Lohri, she was expected to distribute gifts and sweets to all and sundry. In the morning she made a visit to the Gurudwara Sahib and gave alms to all the beggars lined up outside its gate. Then she called all the servants of the palace and gifted a set of new clothes to each of them. Hampers of sweets were sent to the officers and their families who lived within the palace premises. The members of the royal family came last of all. The queen mother called them all to her chamber, blessed them and gifted new clothes and gold ornaments to them. The little prince, whose first Lohri was being celebrated, was given a pair of gold anklets. His mother received an elaborate necklace, a *naulakha haar* – a fitting gift for the mother of the would-be king of Patiala.

Betty had not seen anything like this before. She watched the ongoing preparations and savoured each moment – the vibrancy, the multiple colours beautifying the city, the garlands decorating the trees and bushes, the lights, the bonfire and the sweets. She accompanied Minnie to the Lohri celebrations in the courtyard. They sat on the chairs placed around the fire, some distance away from the rajmata who was seated with the maharani and the little prince. The maharaja was not to be seen. He, along with his inner circle of officers, including Charles Bryan, joined the gathering much later, only when it was time to light the fire and several messengers had been sent to call them. Minnie and Betty guessed that they had privately fortified themselves with Patiala pegs before joining the celebrations.

The occasion demanded that the maharaja should sit with his mother, the rajmata, his wife, the maharani, and their infant son. So he did. Betty saw him hold the child in his arms and play with him. She saw the maharani, dressed in the best of her finery, rise from her seat, cover her head respectfully as he approached, and bow low. The maharaja, acknowledging the gesture, placed his hand benevolently on her head and helped her back into her seat. On the face of it, they were an ideal ruling couple, deferential towards each other. After a while, once the bonfire was lit and the prayers were chanted, the maharaja handed the child back to the queen and walked across towards Minnie. As he approached them, Betty saw the rajmata turn and look in her direction with curiosity. She also saw the maharani eyeing her keenly. Seeing the look in the maharani's eyes, Betty froze. It was a look of hostility, a look of cold dislike, the look of one whose gritted teeth and icy stare told her that there would be trouble ahead. It made Betty's hair stand on end and sent a shiver down her spine.

But the maharaja was now close to them, greeting her and Minnie politely. Betty thought no more of the unnerving hostile glance directed towards her. A group of colourfully dressed singers was singing foot-tapping numbers, the *dholak* playing on the side. Another troupe of young men dressed in traditional outfits, danced to the tune, performing a lively bhangra. The bonfire continued to roar. Sweets and dry fruit were circulated. Caught up in the mirth and laughter, the song and dance, Betty soon forgot her discomfiture. When the younger girls of the palace got up to dance a *giddha*, she spotted Jasbir and Harbir among them. She called out to them and they drew her into the circle of dancers. Betty, incongruous in her long evening dress, dropped her reserve and joined them in the *giddha*. The maharaja looked on with an indulgent smile. His royal consort, the maharani, looked straight ahead, her eyes blank and expressionless.

The Lohri bonfire crackled on. The singing and dancing, eating, drinking and merry-making continued well into the night.

FAMILY MATTERS

The little prince, Bhupinder Singh, had been at his *nankas* with his mother for more than a month now. He was pampered silly by his maternal grandparents, his aunts and uncles. The youngest of his maternal aunts was only eight years old and she spent all her time playing with the infant, much to the consternation of the queen's masseuse, Kulwinder, who had accompanied her royal protégé on this visit and was taking care of the baby. The uncles were older and comparatively more reserved in their show of affection. Dhirendra mamu, the eldest, of the uncles, spent more time with his sister, closeted in the family parlour, talking in low, hushed whispers. This is how Kulwinder sometimes chanced upon them; they seemed to be discussing some matter of utmost importance. Sometimes the maharani's parents would join in the discussion.

What was afoot? Kulwinder was curious and tried to eavesdrop but she was invariably sent away on some errand. Clearly, they were discussing a very secret matter. Sometimes, before they could send her away, she would catch snatches of their conversation. Words and phrases that strayed her way were disjointed and did not make much sense. 'English girl' was one phrase that came up repeatedly in their conversation. And then 'Charles Bryan'. Kulwinder was wise enough to guess what they were talking about. She was satisfied that the news she had given to her queen was being followed up seriously. Sometimes the maharani would lose her cool and talk in a high-pitched tone. Then her brother would pacify her and tell her to remain calm and be patient. On one occasion it was the brother who, in an outraged tone, shouted that they would take revenge. Then it was the parents who pacified the young man and told him that the fight could be won with the use of wit and intelligence. Again they would go into a huddle and continue to talk in whispers.

Often, in the mornings when the prince was being taken care of by his aunt, Kulwinder would have her time to herself and retreat to some quiet corner with her prayer beads in hand. Sometimes her presence would go unnoticed and she would hear more than her mistress would have liked her to.

'Wait for Baisakhi day, behen-ji,' Prince Dhirendra told his sister. 'Everything will be alright.'

'But I do not wish to lose the maharaja,' she responded. 'I want him to come back to me.'

'He will, behen-ji. Just let me work it out. No one will suspect your hand behind it. You will remain with us meanwhile and go back only after Baisakhi, when matters are settled. This way the maharaja will not blame you for what takes place.'

What was being planned? Kulwinder could only guess. It was no doubt something to do with the maharaja's relationship with the Bryans' daughter. She had seen the white-skinned, golden-haired girl from a distance at the Lohri celebration and the way she had joined in the *giddha* with the other girls. In her heart of hearts, although her loyalties lay with the maharani, she grudgingly admitted that the younger woman looked poised and dignified enough to be a queen. In fact, in a half-formed thought, she saw her as the maharaja's chhoti rani. So, was this what the senior maharani was upset about? And what would they do on Baisakhi day? Kulwinder was almost dying of curiosity but she could not possibly ask anyone. So she just resigned herself to the fact that they would be staying on as guests of the Nankas at least for another two months, until after Baisakhi.

'But, meanwhile, behen-ji, we have to keep up appearances. We will not give them any cause to suspect our involvement in whatever happens.'

'But … ,' the maharani was unsure.

'Don't worry, nobody will be harmed. The English girl will go back to wherever she came from. That's what you want, isn't it?'

'Yes, *veera*,' she replied.

'Baba-ji will help us get rid of the firangi and restore your husband to you,' said the maharani's aged father, joining his hands in a gesture of prayer towards a replica of the Golden Temple on the table.

'*Wahe Guru ji da Khalsa, wahe Guru ji di fateh!*' The meeting was over and they dispersed without realising they had been overheard.

What could Kulwinder do? She was excited at the thought that she was now privy to something momentous that was being planned but knew that if she squealed a word to anyone she would be thrown out. So she kept her secret to herself and waited for events to unfold. After all, Baisakhi was not too far off.

Meanwhile, in Patiala, the rajmata thought it was high time she met the maharaja's new love interest. She had deliberately delayed the visit, hoping that her son's affection for the white girl would fizzle out. But when she realised that this was not to be, she decided to go and pay the Bryans a visit. Now that the badi maharani – she too had started thinking of her daughter-in-law as the badi maharani now – was away visiting her parents, it would be less complicated to pay the new one a visit.

Going unannounced was not her style, so she sent a message across to the Bryans during the day that she would visit them in the evening and share dinner with them. As a result, there was general consternation in the Bryan household. The queen mother's visit was not an ordinary event and the Bryans wondered how to receive her in the appropriate manner. However, while they were still in a tizzy, the rajmata sent another message telling them to keep the visit very private and not to make any special preparations.

So it was that a low-key dinner was organised. The matriarch came and went without any fanfare. Just she and a maid-in-waiting, with a sentry escorting them. The maharaja greeted her at the entrance. He looked big, tall and burly next to Betty who stood by his side, like a delicate half-blown rose. The Bryans stood a few feet away. They greeted her with folded hands. The queen mother responded with a polite 'Good evening, Charles; good evening, Minnie. How are you?' and then turned to Betty.

Before she could say another word, Betty had taken a step forward, knelt before the dowager, touched her feet respectfully, and said in a low tone, '*Pairi pauna, beeji.*' She had rehearsed this meeting many times in privacy, learned the appropriate gesture and the correct way of uttering these words to show respect to an elder of the family. The act was flawless. The maharaja, too, was surprised: he had not expected this. In fact, he was worried how Betty would present herself. So were the Bryans taken by surprise. As for the rajmata, she was completely disarmed.

'*Jeendi raho, puttar*,' she placed her hand on the bent head and gestured that she should rise.

Then began a conversation in a slow, halting manner. Rajmata could speak enough English to converse with Betty and Betty had learned enough Punjabi words to get by.

'Would you like to be called Florence or Betty?' was the first question the rajmata put to the young woman.

She replied respectfully: 'Whatever you choose to call me, *beeji*.'

'Ah, then we must think of a suitable name for you. Until then you will remain Florence.'

'Yes, *beeji*.' Betty, or Florence as she was called, was obedience personified. The older woman liked her apparent docility.

Dinner was a pleasant affair. With due respect to the rajmata, no alcoholic drinks were served. Conversation was polite and politically correct. However, once the dinner was over and the servants withdrew, the rajmata, who had seemed somewhat distracted with her own thoughts through the dinner, approached the subject directly. She addressed the Bryans: 'Charles, Minnie,' she said, 'Florence will continue to live with you as your daughter until the nuptials take place.'

Betty and the maharaja exchanged meaningful glances. The rajmata's words indicated an approval of the relationship and a green signal for the impending marriage.

The mother continued: 'We will work out an agreement with the viceroy and Her Majesty, the queen. We will also have to think of a strategy to bring around our own people. Until then we maintain status quo and Florence continues to be with you as your daughter.'

'Yes, rajmata sahiba,' the Bryans replied in unison.

'And you, my child,' she turned to Betty, 'will try and learn more of our customs and traditions. I am happy with what you have learned so far, but do keep it up. Our people would be happy with a queen they can identify with.'

'Yes, *beeji*,' Betty replied respectfully.

'And you, my dear boy,' she turned to her son, the maharaja who wore a broad smile, 'you will take care of my daughter-in-law and see that she does not lack anything.'

'Yes, beeji,' his grin became broader.

Before leaving the apartment the queen mother once again blessed Betty. Unclasping an intricately designed gold *kundan-haar* she wore, she placed it around Betty's neck, kissed her on the forehead, and left.

The visit had been a success by any standards. The Bryans were relieved. Betty and Rajen could now plan the next step. The wheels were beginning to turn. Soon, soon, they would be officially recognised as the king and queen of the state.

What other hurdles did they have to encounter? Yes, the British and the locals. They too would be tackled in due course. Hopefully all this would be done before Betty's condition became too obvious.

IN THE ROYAL PALACE

The season began to change soon after Lohri. The sun rose earlier each day. It reached higher and higher into the sky.

As the evenings became longer, the streets of Patiala were less deserted. Instead of huddling up against the cold in the four walls of their homes, people preferred to venture forth into the city, meet their friends and relatives, socialise a bit more than they used to in the cold weather. Kites started dotting the sky. On Basant Panchami the entire city seemed to be out of doors, celebrating the coming spring and the fresh air. The parks were full of young and old in a festive mood. The sky was full of brightly coloured kites. Following the Basant festival, winter gave way to spring and the earth prepared itself for a fresh coat of green grass and spring flowers. By the end of March, the fragrance of flowers was everywhere in the air. The sky was a bright blue and the trees sprouted fresh green leaves and shoots.

Betty loved the smell of the chameli that pervaded the garden where she walked every morning after the maharaja went back to his rooms. This was a secluded private space behind the Bryans' apartment. She loved this corner and enjoyed this peaceful hour to herself, walking barefoot in the dewy grass every morning. Then she would sit on a bench under the champak tree and wait. Soon a squirrel would hop along, inquisitively looking for an early morning meal. Betty would throw some bread crumbs in its direction. Then the sparrows would come, the pigeons and the jackdaws, also demanding their share. The last to come were the green long-tailed parrots that would gracefully swoop down, pick up a morsel and fly off again. Betty would scatter crumbs in different directions. The smaller birds would feed on her left, the bigger ones on the right. She wondered why. Perhaps there was some kind of hierarchy in the bird kingdom, an unwritten code of conduct that they followed.

From the bench on which she sat she could see a huge peepal tree on the far end of the garden. It was reputed to be at least a hundred years old and Betty was fascinated by it. It was like a whole world in itself, a mini kingdom with all kinds of creatures living in it. It had a massive trunk, enormous gnarled branches spreading out in all directions. Invariably she would see squirrels racing up and down, playing peek-a-boo in the knots and twists of the peepal. On the topmost branches was a big nest that she could see only when the foliage was not too thick. Now, with the coming of spring, new green leaves and shoots partially obstructed her view. This was an eagle's nest. Sometimes Betty would see a big bird circling gracefully above the tree before descending to its home in the branches. A few branches below was another nest on the east side of the tree. Here Betty would sometimes see long-legged birds, quite like egrets, flying in at dusk. There were also parrots but she could not figure out where they had their nesting space. In the same way, she had no idea where the jackdaws and the sparrows had their hideouts. The pigeons did not live on the peepal; they had several nests in the deep niches of the outer walls of the palace building. She could hear their guttural chatter throughout the day on the ventilators and the high windows.

On the lowest level of the tree, in the hollow of a thick branch, she knew there lived an owl family. The hollow was like a little cave and Betty wondered how far into the depths of the branch it extended. Two of the owls who lived there were regular fixtures on the branch, sitting at the mouth of the hollow. Sometimes two little owlets could also be seen perched beside them. They would look down at Betty with unblinking eyes. She felt that they were not afraid of her, that they accepted her as one of them. Sitting there, under the champak tree, looking on at the bigger peepal tree, she tried to keep as still as possible so as not to frighten them away. These owls, supposedly night birds, would sit outside their hollow all day long, flying out only after dusk.

And then there were those rabbits that scampered around the tree, nibbling away at the crumbs the birds had left behind. Betty would watch them quietly – the twitching of their nose and the fidgeting of their movements. They would then disappear in burrows hidden somewhere in the grass. Once she had seen a couple of monkeys swinging on the branches. They were noisy and destructive. The owl family had quickly disappeared into their hole when they came around. The other birds had made themselves scarce. The monkeys had vandalised the mango tree in the garden before coming to the swing on the peepal tree. Betty, feeling unsafe in their presence, had quickly retreated within the house.

This is how her mornings were spent in quiet contemplation, in the midst of the greenery of the garden. She would walk around in a leisurely manner, looking at the fresh buds in bloom, the full blown roses, and the rich green grass. Sometimes she would pick a few flowers for the vase on her desk. Or a few jasmine blossoms that she would keep in a bowl full of water. She liked the faint fragrance that would soon spread through the room.

Baisakhi preparations were beginning in the royal city. Betty did not understand the implication of this festival. Again, it was her companions, Jasbir and Harbir, who enlightened her.

Playfully, affectionately, in a sing-song manner, like a duet, each chipping in, a sentence at a time.

Betty commented after listening to them intently: 'So it is a religious festival, and also related to agriculture?'

'And to culture and to the change of seasons,' Harbir continued.

'After Baisakhi the weather starts getting hot and uncomfortable.'

Betty had not experienced the Indian summer yet but she had heard about it. She had been told that the heat became unbearable and it was hard to get out of doors. Calcutta had been unbearably hot, she remembered. That was why the British officers in India would move their families to the cool climes of the Himalayas, Simla being their favourite summer place. Betty wondered where they would go this coming summer. After all, Simla would be out of question now. Would the Chail Palace be ready in the next couple of months? But, in any case, they would stick around in Patiala until Baisakhi. Hopefully it would not get too hot by then.

That night, when Rajen visited her she repeated her conversation with her companions to him and asked him more about Baisakhi.

He nodded and said, 'There's more to it than simply singing and dancing and the Baisakhi mela. The Baisakhi festival has tremendous significance in the Sikh world. We celebrate the festival as a collective birthday of Guru Gobind Singh, the tenth Sikh Guru, and the foundation of the Khalsa Panth, that is, the Sikh brotherhood. Sikhs all over the world celebrate the day with a lot of enthusiasm and joy. The date of Baisakhi has major astrological significance as it marks the sun's entry into Mesh Rashi. That is the next sign of the zodiac.'

She was sitting at her dressing table, brushing her hair. She wore a light cotton nightdress, the colour of her hair. It flattered her complexion and made her eyes look a deeper blue in the lamplight. Rajen came and stood behind her, his hands on her shoulders, looking at the reflection in the glass.

Betty listened carefully. Then she said: 'I will come with you to the gurudwara on Baisakhi day.'

If Rajen was surprised he did not show it. All he said was, 'All right, if you wish.'

'In summer, does it get very hot here in Patiala?' she asked after a pause.

'Hm-mm,' he responded absentmindedly as he played with the soft gold tresses that fell loose about her shoulders. 'But we will go to our palace in Chail. It will be ready by then.'

'After Baisakhi?' she asked.

'Okay, if you wish to stay on until then.'

He was now playing with a green satin ribbon on her dress, twirling it around his finger. Betty finished brushing her hair, looked at his face in the mirror, and saw the half-smile on his face.

She looked up at him and asked: 'What makes my lord smile?'

Still smiling, he replied: 'See for yourself: the beauty and the beast.' He pointed to the mirror.

She followed his gaze and laughed. Rajen was not wearing his turban. He had loosened his hair and his beard. The image in the mirror was of a burly, hirsute man standing next to a frail woman with fair complexion, blonde hair and blue eyes.

She got up and faced him squarely. Taking both his hands in hers, she said, 'Yes, but some beauties actually *like* beasts. So there....'

He sighed contentedly, 'Yes, I am a lucky man, I guess.'

Betty's desire to attend the Baisakhi celebrations was neither spontaneous nor impulsive. She had been seriously mulling over the matter the last few days. A well-deliberated plan was taking shape in her mind and she had decided to implement it on Baisakhi day at the Gurudwara Sahib.

She asked her companions, Harbir and Jasbir to help her get appropriate clothes made for the Baisakhi festival. Delighted to help, they went about their job enthusiastically. They even volunteered to get her matching accessories. The royal *darziani* of the palace, who was called in to take Betty's measurements, helped Betty choose the cloth material carefully. Betty ordered typically Punjabi-style salwar-kameez suits to be stitched. Matching jewellery was ordered. A brocade bag, golden *juttis* and a colourful *paraanda* completed the effect.

Betty was still not satisfied. 'Teach me,' she entreated her companions, 'how to say prayers in Punjabi.' They obliged. Haltingly, Betty learned how to recite '*Ek onkar* ... .'

Then she asked them to give her Punjabi translations of a few sentences. It became more of a game for the three of them. She would give them a sentence or a phrase, they would translate it and she would transcribe it in English in her little red diary. Although the companions thought it was nothing but a game, Betty was very serious about it. More serious than they could ever imagine.

That night in her diary she wrote:

It is almost five months since I came to Patiala. Although I am comfortable here with the Brijans, I can't go on living like this, in this uncertainty.

I think it is high time I moved into the palace proper.

Rajen, too wants to hasten events but something is holding him back. I think he is afraid of something. But what? The rajmata seems to like me. I don't think there will be any opposition from her side. Perhaps it is the badi maharani that they are apprehensive of. But she has been at her parents' home for the last month and more, not likely to return for another few months, so I am told.

I think I know the reason. Rajen and his mother, the rajmata, are both afraid of the common people and how they will react to the idea of having an alien woman for their queen. The Sikhs are a proud community. They will not relish the idea of a foreign woman installing herself as a queen in their state. So how can I expect them to accept me as their queen?

Sitting at this desk, leaning over the table, I can feel a churning in my belly. The baby is growing within me and feels constricted. Rajen's baby and mine needs more space. I too need more space. I need to change my situation. I must think, think hard. What kind of a world do I want my child to come into? I must bring him into a home that is rightfully his, rightfully ours. Into a friendly environment where he has a legitimate place, into a world that is ready to accept him.

She got up from the table, walked up and down the room. Outside the long windows overlooking the garden she could see the sky changing colours with the setting sun. The horizon was tinged with pink and orange. Almost red. Back home in England, the red sky at night was a signal for rain the following morning: 'Red sky at night, the shepherd's delight. Red sky in the morning, the shepherd's warning.'

The old superstition of the English countryside echoed in her head. Apparently it did not hold good here in Punjab because lately almost every day the evening sky had been reddish but the mornings that followed were clear, not rainy.

Betty did not miss her home in England. Nor did she miss her life with her parents in Calcutta and in Simla. Caught up in the novelty of experiences in Patiala, she had little time for brooding or reminiscing. Uppermost in her mind was the answer that she was seeking – how would she make the people of Patiala accept her as their queen.

She went out into the garden, paced up and down for a while and then sat on the stone bench. The sky had darkened and one single star twinkled in the distance. Inadvertently she brought her fingertips together, moved her hands back and forth, started rubbing her nails, the right fingernails against the left, muttering, 'Star light, star bright, the first star I see tonight, I wish I may, I wish I might....'

Now what could she wish for? Betty took a deep breath, made a silent wish and said a quiet prayer. She then rose and took a turn in the garden, still in deep thought. In the peepal tree above there was a cacophony of birds but she did not pay much attention to it. The chatter of the seven sisters settling in for the night, the high-pitched cry of the eagle as it circled over its nest, the dull screech of the owl as it scurried into its hole in the tree trunk, hiding from the eagle, the pigeons and the parrots, all of them competed with each other, adding to the late-evening noises. Betty walked up and down, concentrated on the pavement, a slight frown creasing her forehead. When something suddenly whooshed past her head and she heard the whirr of a bat's wing, she realised she should go indoors again. Rajen would be coming in any time now.

Her thoughts had cleared. Back at her desk, she sat at her diary again and wrote: *I must get them to accept me as one of them, not as a foreigner.*

She paused thoughtfully, chewing the end of her pen. Then she continued:

The people of Patiala are honest, robust and large-hearted. They will accept me if I am honest with them. I must convince them of my sincerity first. How do I do that? How do I make them accept me?

A footstep outside told her of Rajen's arrival. She closed the notebook, put it away in the drawer, rose and went to the door to receive the maharaja.

So it happened that Betty, like the badi maharani, but for different reasons, also waited impatiently for Baisakhi. Whereas the maharani's reasons were motivated by hate and envy, in her keenness to get rid of someone who was a thorn in her side trying to usurp her place, Betty's reasons related to love for the maharaja and the desire to be part of his world. The maharani was confident that her plans would succeed and the white girl would be sent back to where she belonged. Betty was apprehensive and could not leave anything to chance. It was an opportunity that she could not afford to miss. Nothing should go wrong.

She sought a meeting with the rajmata and requested her for permission to accompany her to the gurudwara. The rajmata did not ask any questions. She kept her own counsel but told Betty that she, along with the Bryans, could go with her and the maharaja to the Baisakhi celebrations.

'But,' she said, 'you need to cover your heads, so take some scarves with you.'

'Yes, *beeji*,' Betty was delighted.

Rajen met his mother a few days later. They talked about Betty and he reminded her that marriage plans should be finalised now. It was essential because Betty's condition was now delicate. She was now going to be a mother. Another prince was on his way. It was now imperative that Betty should be installed as the chhoti maharani without further delay.

'But what about the viceroy?' she asked. 'This will complicate matters, won't it?'

'On the contrary, it may lead us to a solution.' He paused and then added: 'Once the baby comes the picture will change and they may be more amenable to a truce.'

The rajmata did not seem convinced but she remained silent.

A CELEBRATION WITH A WEDDING

A week before Baisakhi, Betty's bubbly companions, Jasbir and Harbir, could hardly contain their excitement. They came to Betty one morning, chirping and chattering merrily, like a pair of jackdaws. The reason, they told Betty amidst high-pitched excitement, was the addition of a new member in their family following the marriage of their brother.

'So suddenly? Without prior notice?' asked Betty.

'Yes, he lives in Amritsar. Attar *veer-ji* is our big brother. He liked a girl who lived in the neighbourhood. She is not from a Sikh family and her parents did not agree. So they quietly got married in the gurudwara. This happened two months ago and he didn't even tell us. But now he's brought her to Patiala to visit us,' Harbir informed her.

'And she's so pretty! Our bhabhi is fair like you. But you have blue eyes and hers are greenish-blue with a shade of brown,' added Jasbir.

'So many colours?' asked Betty in surprise.

'Yes, and they seem to change colour. In the morning they are different. At noon they are darker.'

'Very unusual,' said Betty.

'You must meet her, madam,' they both cried in unison.

'Yes, I will,' responded Betty.

Attar Singh, a young Sikh married to a Hindu girl. The story made Betty think. It was parallel to her story and yet different. Both, Attar and his bride, were from the same background and so their case was not as complicated as hers.

She sighed and put the thought out of her mind. A solution would surely be found. She decided to remain optimistic.

And finally it was Baisakhi. Betty woke up in the morning with butterflies in her stomach. The baby was moving inside her and she rushed to the basin to throw up. It was still dark when Rajen had left her side, reminding her to get dressed well in time. The royal household would make their appearance at the gurudwara shortly before midday when the maximum number of people gathered there. There they would all pay obeisance, and then make their presence felt at the community meal, the *langar* that the rajmata organised on every festival. Then, as was the custom, the maharaja along with the other members of the royal family, would appear on the public platform at the main entrance, address the public and give donations to the poor people assembled at the gates. The entire population of Patiala would converge on the scene. The young and the old, the frail and the weak, infants in the arms of their mothers, the poor, the lame and the crippled, all would turn up, line up for the *langar* or to hear the short speech that the maharaja would address to the public.

This Baisakhi would be just the same. The only difference was that the maharani was away to her *maike*. There was nothing unusual about it in the opinion of the public. Perhaps she was in the family way again, some people speculated, and so needed parental care. Therefore, on this occasion the maharaja, accompanied by his mother, would follow the custom without the maharani.

Baisakhi celebrations had always witnessed a heavy turnout at the gurudwara but this time the number present in the courtyard and in the *maidan* opposite the holy shrine was far larger than the usual. There were the devotees within the gurudwara, scattered groups of people thronging the compound, vendors at temporary stalls outside, some urchins squatting at the gate and some old people labouring up the stairs.

Jasbir and Harbir came with their parents. They were accompanied by their brother, Attar Singh, and his new bride. Together, they came as a family to bow before the holy shrine and seek the Guru's blessings. The new bride was dressed in her bridal finery, a deep crimson salwar-kameez. Red and white bangles glistened on her wrists. Her head was covered with a golden dupatta under which a *tikka* glowed on her forehead. She was striking in appearance, her loveliness made even more attractive by the smile of contentment on her face. What was most remarkable, however, was the colour of her eyes. On this particular morning they were the colour of the sea – an aquamarine colour, deep and rich. When she looked around wonderstruck at the huge throngs of people her eyes widened even more and seemed to reflect the colour of the sky. Jasbir and Harbir were proud of their sister-in-law and introduced her to all their acquaintances. Attar Singh, escorting them, stood by, tall and reticent, an indulgent half-smile on his face as his sisters giggled and fussed over his wife. The gurudwara was an excellent place for socialising. Relatives and friends would catch up with each other's lives in the courtyard or over the *langar*. This Baisakhi, in particular, there was much catching up to do and Attar's sisters were making the best use of the opportunity.

Amid conversations and cross-conversations the hubbub seemed to increase steadily. By the time the sun was well up in the sky the precincts of the gurudwara had become unusually noisy. Jasbir wondered why. Something seemed to be not quite normal. She looked around and saw that there was a lot of commotion on the other side of the road where the Baisakhi mela was being held. What was happening? They all wondered. Instructing the girls to wait in a corner, Attar Singh went to inquire.

The Baisakhi mela was an annual affair. Swings and ferris wheels were regular features. So were puppet shows, food stalls and a number of other forms of entertainment. This time, however, the sounds of entertainment were being drowned by some unruly slogans. There seemed to be a large group of people – perhaps a hundred or more – who were clearly not there for fun or entertainment or worship. They were all dressed in similar fashion – white kurta pyjamas, with a blue turban on the head, flowing beard, *kirpan* hanging by the side and an orange scarf across the shoulders. Their demeanour was belligerent. The air was volatile. Attar Singh fearlessly walked towards them to find out what the problem was.

They did not seem to be the local gentry. The conversation he overheard was full of hate and aggression. It was evident that this was a hired brigade that had come to the venue deliberately to make mischief. But what kind of mischief? Getting closer, Attar noted that some of the men carried spears. As they talked angrily, they prodded the ground with the butt-end of the spears, giving ample evidence of the seething anger within. Seeing one of them standing on the margins of the crowd, more of an onlooker than an anarchist, Attar walked up to him and made discreet inquiries.

'What is it, brother? What is the trouble about?'

'They have come to protest. They are against the maharaja,' the man replied. 'He should stay away from firangis.'

'What do you mean?' Attar asked.

'That firangi woman he has been seeing. She is not one of us. She is alien. He should send her back or else there will be trouble,' it was a studied response, cold and calculated. And rigid.

The people were getting restless. They were still waiting for the maharaja who had not yet arrived. Just then a horseman, evidently one of them, rode up to tell them that the royal carriage was approaching. It was a signal of sorts. A war-cry broke out in unison and the air was filled with slogans. Together, the blue-turbaned men raised their spears and shouted slogans. They were slogans of unity against all invaders, against all foreigners, against all those who would dare betray the sanctity, purity and integrity of the state of Patiala.

Attar Singh hurried back to where the rest of his family waited, huddled under an arch, wondering what the sudden tumult was all about. The excitement and bonhomie among other people in the courtyard had evaporated. A cloud of uneasiness hovered over them as they all turned to look at the disturbance across the road. The maharaja's carriage could now be seen rolling down towards the gurudwara. The throngs on both sides of the road stood waiting. On one side of the road there was a hushed, anxious silence. On the other, a hostile crowd shouting slogans edged in closer and stood in a semicircle near the steps leading to the gurudwara.

A collective shout ran through the slogan-shouting crowd when the royal carriages drew up at the main entrance of the gurudwara. Usually it was a single carriage but this time there were two of them. The first carriage carried the rajmata and her son, the maharaja. The second one bore the Bryans and Betty. The roar of the crowd rose to a deafening crescendo as the rajmata and the maharaja descended. It continued unabated as the Bryans alighted from their carriage. Betty was the last to emerge from the carriage. As she stepped down from the carriage, a collective gasp ran through the mass of people. She was not attired in her usual long dress and bonnet. Instead she sported a red silk salwar-kameez. A matching red and gold dupatta was draped over her head and shoulders. Her hair was braided and a red *paraanda* dangled over her back. On each of her wrists she wore a dozen red and golden bangles. Her feet were shod in brocade *juttis*. She was dressed every bit like a Punjaban. Her fair complexion glowed a healthy pink. Her eyes were downcast. With her head covered, she looked like a demure Sikh bride.

The slogans that were rending the air seemed to peter out suddenly. A hush descended on the crowd that had gathered there to protest against her presence in the palace. Spears and swords that were raised in hostility seemed to freeze mid-air. With Charles and Minnie, Betty walked up to the maharaja and his mother. She respectfully touched the matriarch's feet and together they began moving towards the main entrance of the gurudwara. At the bottom of the stairs, Betty, like the others, went down on her knees and touched the ground with her forehead.

The silence in the courtyard was almost palpable.

On the topmost stair, the maharaja and the rajmata turned to face the crowd. The maharaja raised his right hand, acknowledging the presence of the people, and was about to address them when Betty touched his elbow lightly and asked for permission to speak to the public. He was too surprised to react; she turned and faced the crowd. Folding her hands, she bowed her head. Then, as the maharaja, the rajmata, the Bryans and all the others looked on in surprise, wondering what she was up to, she held up the hem of her dupatta in both hands in a gesture of supplication and addressed the gathering: *'Patiala de jaandar te khoobsoorat niwasiyon …'*

The silence in the gurudwara precincts was almost deafening.

She continued, her voice resounding loud and clear: *'Main tuhade wich rehna chahundi han. Eh meri sachche dil di awaaz hai.*

Sachche dil nal meri ik benti hai ki tussi meinu pyar naal apna samjho te apna kabool karo.' I wish to be yours, she had said; with all sincerity I beg you to accept me as your own.

The drop of a pin could be heard in the silence that followed. With her dupatta held out to the crowd, she stood silent with her head bowed before them. Several seconds passed and then a lone voice from the crowd shouted, *'Wahe Guru ji da khalsa ... .'*

A pause and then someone else answered, *'Wahe Guru ji di fateh.'*

It was apparently the leader of the hostile crowd who was striding towards the maharaja. Coming closer, he muttered something in a low tone. The maharaja nodded, exchanged a whispered dialogue with Betty and turned to the public.

Addressing them in the local dialect, he said: 'My dear fellowmen, you seem to be annoyed because you think I am courting a foreigner. But, believe me, she is one of us. She wishes to embrace our faith. And I wish to marry her. Will you accept her as a sardarni? And as your queen?'

A momentary silence and then the leader of the rebel group gestured towards his people and answered loudly on their behalf: 'Yes, maharaj. If she should embrace our faith we have no objections if you marry her. We will accept her as our queen.'

The air resounded with cries of *'Maharaj di jai'.*

Then, *'Bole sonehal sat siri akal!'*

And then a lone shrill cry went up: *'Chhoti maharani di jai.'* The cry was taken up by the people. It was repeated over and over again. The threat of insurrection had passed. Betty had been accepted as the chhoti maharani. So sudden, so unexpected, it was nothing short of a miracle.

A semblance of normalcy having returned to the scene, conversations began again. Vendors resumed their trade and the giant wheel of the fair started going round once more. The leader of the sloganeers continued talking to the maharaja and then returned to his people on the other side of the road. No one could explain the sudden change of heart. It was unbelievable. But the results were happy and no one in the gathering complained.

Peace descended once more as the maharaja addressed the gathering: 'My people, this is your new maharani, Bibi Harnam Kaur. From today she is a sardarni. In the presence of all gathered here, she will take the Sikh vows and become one of us. In the presence of all my people I will marry her. Call the *granthi.*'

He snapped his fingers and a guard went running to call the priest. Taking Betty by the hand, Rajen walked up to the inner hall of the gurudwara. Both of them knelt before the Guru Granth Sahib and then sat down cross-legged, facing the priest, waiting for him to conduct the ceremonies, initiate Betty into the Sikh faith and then pronounce them man and wife.

The rajmata looked on serenely as arrangements were quickly made for an *anand-kaaraj.* Minnie, quite overcome with the suddenness of events, pulled out a lacey handkerchief from her pocket and snivelled into it. Jasbir and Harbir, who were actually on their way out, came right back with their brother and bhabi to witness the royal wedding. The maharaja and his new bride completed all the rituals, gave alms in charity to the poor, and came back to the palace. This time Betty did not need to go to the Bryans' apartment. She accompanied the maharaja and his mother to the main palace as the royal bride, the new chhoti maharani as she would henceforth be called.

Back in her parents' home, the badi maharani's sorrow knew no bounds when she heard what had transpired. The *jattha* sent by her brothers had fizzled out. They had assured her that the plan would not fail. But apparently the English girl had outsmarted them. She had pulled the rug from under their feet, taken them all by surprise and was now installed as the royal consort. So what could be done? Nothing much, the maharani realised. She would just lie low and wait for another opportunity. This time she would not ask her brothers to help. She would pick her own brains and find a solution. But first she would have to eat humble pie and go back to the palace where her rightful place had been usurped by another. She would have to remain in the margins and watch her husband making merry with her *soukan*.

Betty's diary entry for the day went thus:

Baisakhi. This has been a red letter day for me. The Sikhs are a large-hearted people. I pleaded with them and they have accepted me. I embraced their faith and they gave me their maharaja. I am now his legally wedded wife. No longer am I Betty or even Florence. I am now Bibi Harnam Kaur, the second wife of Rajinder Singh, Maharaja of Patiala.

This is the greatest gift I could possibly get. I love my city. I love my people. I pledge my loyalty to them, forever and ever.

A few days after Rani Harnam Kaur was formally installed in the main palace she wanted to meet her companions again. The last few days had been so busy that she had not given them a thought. But once the dust settled on the event she began to miss those playful mornings with Jasbir and Harbir. Why had they forsaken her? On making enquiries she was told that they were busy with their new sister-in-law, getting new clothes and jewellery made for her. After all, she had left her parents' home with little but the clothes she wore. Attar had managed to get her a few dresses but she needed a whole new wardrobe and her young and vivacious sisters-in-law were helping her in the task.

Betty comprehended the scenario very well. The rajmata was doing exactly the same thing for her, getting the *darziani* come in every day to take her measurements for new clothes befitting a maharani, bringing in the jeweller with fresh samples of ornaments, and supervising other details that Betty needed to be initiated into. Even so, Betty sent a message for her companions and they turned up one afternoon, their usual selves, giggly and spontaneous. They told her how much they were enjoying the visit of their *veer-ji* and bhabi. But soon they would return to Amritsar, they informed her with a touch of sadness. Their brother, Attar Singh had to go back to his job. Bhabi would go too.

Before Attar Singh left for Amritsar he visited the maharaja and Betty with his bride. The royal couple received them graciously and made polite conversation. The maharaja had a special soft corner for Attar Singh, both having grown up together in the precincts of the old fort of Patiala. Bonds of childhood were strong and the warmth between the two was palpable.

Attar Singh bowed low before the maharaja. Placing his right hand on his heart he said feelingly, 'Maharaj, if I can ever be of service to you, please do not hesitate. I am always at your disposal.'

The maharaja thumped him on the back, wished him luck and they parted.

VICEREGAL CONNECTIONS

As the seasons changed the sun became hotter and hotter. Betty, now Harnam Kaur or the chhoti maharani, found the heat unbearable so the maharaja made plans to move her to the new palace at Chail.

Meanwhile, the viceroy and the British governmental paraphernalia returned again to romance with Simla. Summer frolics began once more – the picnics and the parties, the banquets and the balls. The Viceregal Lodge was once again the centre of social activities but they were comparatively subdued this year. Last year's notorious episode still lingered in the minds of the people although no one talked about it. A veil of secrecy was thrown over the whole episode. It was as though it never took place. Privately, however, small groups continued to speculate on the outcome, on what must have happened and what would now happen. But there was no way of finding out. The viceroy and his wife were mum on the subject. Their staff at the lodge knew nothing about it. So the story was never made public. Those who had actually witnessed it had repeated it a million times and with every narration a new twist, a fresh detail, newly-minted in the imagination of the narrator, was added to the elopement so that eventually even the eyewitnesses were not sure of what they had really seen.

Nobody got to know when the viceroy sent another messenger to Patiala asking the maharaja one more time to return their daughter. Nobody was told that the maharaja had declined again. Instead, he had invited the viceregal couple to visit their daughter in the royal city and assured them of due respect and courtesy. No one knew of the closed-door debates that went on between the viceroy and his wife or of their final decision to go to Patiala. One early morning two closed carriages rolled out of the Viceregal Lodge, accompanied by a small posse of soldiers and headed downhill for the plains. The viceroy and his wife were going to meet their daughter after more than six months. God willing, they would bring her back with them.

Patiala was a totally new experience for the viceroy and his wife. The city wore a festive air, decorated with flowers and garlands. At the main entrance of the palace they received a traditional welcome with *diyas* and flowers, with songs of welcome sung by a choir of women. They were feeling hot and tired, having covered a long distance and so were taken to the guest apartments to freshen up and rest for a while before meeting the maharaja and his new bride, their daughter. Meanwhile, there were servants, maids and *durbans* to see to their comfort. The royal couple, so they were told, would join them over tea shortly.

Tea took place in an elaborate dining hall, brought in by a row of handmaids, each bearing a silver tray laden with fresh fruit, dry fruit, sweets and snacks. As the viceroy and his wife waited for their daughter to join them, they sauntered around looking at the decorations on the walls and the ceiling, the portraits looking down at the splendour of the dining hall, its rich golden columns and arches, the ornamental statues in the corners, a waterfall in the midst of the hall, trickling a steady stream into a pool in which goldfish swam. The floor itself was inlaid with marble and reflected the lengthening rays of the sun that streamed in from the windows. A faint fragrance pervaded the hall, from incense burning discreetly in the hidden niches of the walls. Here was royalty at its best. An aesthetic blend of rich splendour and refined taste.

A whisper ran through the waiting servants lined up along the far end of the room. The maharaja and his new wife had arrived.

The maharaja was in his ceremonial clothes, dressed in his entire splendour, displaying a lot of gold, pearls and jewels on his person. He walked with confidence, a slight smile on his face, his back straight, shoulders pushed back, chest out. On his right arm leaned a woman who was again dressed in ceremonial Punjabi clothes – a pale green salwar-kameez with silver sequins all over, her head and half her face covered with a translucent lacey veil which was draped lightly over her shoulders. Around her neck glittered a multicoloured bejewelled necklace that hugged her throat and extended down to the neckline of her dress. Matching earrings dangled in each ear, bangles clinked softly on her delicate wrists. She walked into the room leaning on the maharaja's arm, her face half-hidden from public view. With each step that she took the anklets and toe-rings she wore made a faint tinkling sound. Bejewelled sandals on her feet glinted under the hem of her salwar.

At first the viceroy and his wife did not recognise their daughter. When Betty lifted her veil and showed her face, the older woman gasped and ran to her.

'Betty, my darling, it's you!' she hugged her close and wept.

Betty's eyes were moist, too, but she controlled herself.

'Hush, mother,' Betty whispered into her mother's ear. 'This is no time to weep.'

She clapped her hands and signalled to the servants to leave the room. Once they were by themselves she turned to her father who stood looking on uncertainly, dumbstruck by the change he saw in his daughter.

'Father, how are you?' she went up to him and took his hands in hers.

The viceroy was swallowing hard. He managed to smile and say, 'Fine, dear child, with God's grace. We have been so worried about you!'

'I am happy, dear father, please do not worry on my account.'

Her mother spoke again, 'Oh, why did you do this to us, my child?'

Betty turned to her mother and held her close, 'Mother, I have simply chosen my life partner. What's wrong with that? I love him and care for him. He loves me too. You can see how happy he has made me.'

The maharaja stood quietly, watching the exchange. The viceroy made a visible effort to control himself. His wife still sobbed, 'O, Betty, Betty.'

Betty spoke again, 'I am not Betty now, mother. I am Rani Harnam Kaur. You gave birth to me, I agree, but now I belong here. This is my husband. These are my people. They love me and I will never leave them.' She pulled herself up erectly as she spoke with a quiet dignity.

Her mother suddenly looked down and noticed the slight bump in her daughter's belly. She took her aside and whispered, 'You are in the family way, my child?'

'Yes,' said Betty. 'I am expecting a little prince. You will be grandparents soon.'

They moved to a seating arrangement in the corner and sat down. Betty continued to hold her mother's hands in hers throughout the conversation. Opposite them sat the maharaja and the viceroy. At first there seemed to be some discomfort in their communication but the maharaja was adept at putting people at ease. He soon got the viceroy talking – first about the weather, then the city of Patiala, and finally about the British rulers sojourning in Simla. They spoke in low tones without any hostility. The viceroy tried to explain to the maharaja that he, being a representative of the English monarch, could not possibly approve of the marriage or even consider it valid. It would be a politically incorrect step to take. In fact he had actually come with the intention of forcibly taking his daughter back with him but now he wondered if it was a good idea, seeing how well-adjusted she was in her new surroundings, and how radiant she looked as the queen of Patiala. When he noticed the beginnings of the baby bump, he began to view the entire situation in a different light. How could he take back his daughter when she was preparing to be a mother soon? How would he explain it to his friends and family? How would they take it? No, the entire issue needed re-thinking. He would discuss it with his wife. They would talk to Betty on a serious note and find out what she wanted. Then they would negotiate with the maharaja who was now their son-in-law and finally they would have to reason with Her Majesty, the Queen of England, explaining the complexity of the situation to Her Highness. For now, there was little choice before them. They would simply have to bide their time and accept the situation.

Time. Betty's parents needed time to absorb all that they had seen and experienced in Patiala. They needed to arrive at a rational approach. Here was their daughter whom they wanted back at any cost. But now her life was entwined with other lives. So what were they to do? In the long hours of the still night, after the royal couple had left, the viceroy and his wife strolled in the jasmine-scented garden and discussed matters secretively. They weighed the pros and cons. Should they leave their daughter behind and annoy the Queen of England? Or should they take her back? In the latter case they would not only destroy their child's happiness but also face social ostracism from their immediate circle.

Exhausted, finally, the viceroy sighed, 'Tomorrow is another day. We will call it a day now, sleep over the matter and reopen it at breakfast.'

Breakfast in the morning was hosted by the rajmata. She sat at the head of the table, elegant and dignified in her usual cream silk salwar-kameez, her head covered with an embroidered dupatta. The only jewellery she wore was a twisted gold chain around her neck and plain gold studs in her ears. The maharaja sat on her right, polite and deferential. Next to him was Betty. Her mother, sitting across the table, noted that she looked a bit wan early in the morning. Perhaps she was nauseous because of her condition. But Betty was smiling cheerfully and seemed to be happy.

A serious exchange took place between the viceroy and the rajmata who seemed to understand exactly what Betty's parents were going through. She was patient and considerate, and explained to them that their daughter was now Rani Harnam Kaur with a life of her own. They should realise and respect this reality.

'Children have to grow up and fly the bird's nest one day,' said the rajmata. 'Don't grudge them their separate lives.'

The viceroy nodded thoughtfully: 'Yes, madam, but the political fallout. That is what worries me.'

'I understand very well,' she replied gently, 'but we have to find a way to overcome the problem. My people have accepted their new queen. The ball is in your court now. You have to work out on how you will resolve the issue with your queen.'

Betty followed the conversation anxiously. She was relieved that the discussion was civil, and that there was understanding and empathy between the two parties. Thank heavens, the earlier animosity had evaporated! Soon, she hoped, all would be well.

And then the viceroy addressed the maharaja directly: 'I am afraid, young man, we will not be able to invite you to Simla any more.'

This was his parting shot.

The maharaja smiled politely, 'No need, sir. I shall invite you to my palace not far from Simla. Do visit us there. We will be going to our Chail Palace in the coming weeks. The heat in the plains is getting too oppressive for my queen.' He placed a protective arm around Betty's shoulder.

SOJOURN IN THE HILLS

Chail was a dream come true. Betty leaned back in her chair on the lush green lawn and looked up at the clear blue sky. It was even better than Simla. It was her idea of paradise. The salubrious climate was good for her and she looked healthy and rosy. As the baby inside her grew, she became rounded and her features acquired a softer, more serene expression. She spent leisurely hours walking around in the garden or resting on the chairs placed under a multicoloured umbrella on the lawn. Rajen would sit with her sometimes and watch her nimble fingers at work as she knitted colourful booties and caps for the expected baby. After a late lunch Betty would go indoors to rest and Rajen would head for the cricket field to have a game with some of his officers. True to his word, he had created a cricket pitch on the highest point in Chail by simply levelling off the top of a high hill. Surrounded by willow trees which had recently been planted by his gardeners, this pitch was undoubtedly the highest in the world.

The hill on which the palace stood was called Rajgarh Hill. It had two other companion hills, one on either side. One was the Pandhewa Hill which housed an officer of the British Empire in charge of the State of Patiala. The third, the Sidh Hill, was crowned by a temple known as the 'Sidh Baba ka Mandir'. Originally this was the hill where the maharaja wished to build his palace. But superstitions prevailing in the region warned him against tampering with the hill. Disregarding the advice of the local residents, he had in fact given orders for construction on the spot but a series of mishaps had forced him to change his mind. First, two of the labourers working on the site were bitten by a poisonous snake; next, there was an unexpected cloudburst followed by a landslide when the excavation was about to begin. Finally, when the maharaja was debating whether or not to give credence to the local beliefs, he had a strange dream at night: a mendicant appeared to him and told him that the hill which he was trying to desecrate actually belonged to a sage who had meditated on the spot and whose remains were now interred in the soil. Constructing or digging on the spot would mean disturbing the soul of the sage and the maharaja was advised against doing so. Bowing before these omens, Maharaja Rajinder Singh moved his workers away from Sidh Hill and they began to work on the one that now housed the palace. Next, he got the famous cricket and polo grounds constructed, the highest in the world, at a height of more than eight thousand feet above sea level. The palace itself stood at a height of seven thousand three hundred feet, which was a good three hundred feet higher than Simla.

This was the maharaja's reaction to his banishment from the British summer capital: this was his answer to the imperial power. Just a year ago there was little to boast of in Chail. It was just another sleepy little hamlet in the hills, the poor cousin of favoured spots like Kasauli and Simla. But the royal house of Patiala had acquired it some years ago and now the maharaja had it built in record time. This was his first summer in the newly-built palace with his much-loved Betty. From here, they could look down at the Simla hills visible in the far distance on a clear day. On clear nights a faint glow along the skyline outlined the location of the British summer capital, the place where their story had first begun.

On this particular day, as they sat on an especially installed wrought-iron swing under the willow tree in the front lawn, admiring the immaculately maintained rows of dahlias, Betty was on a nostalgic trip. She was telling Rajen of her childhood in England, of the games she played as a child, the nursery rhymes she still remembered. One hand rested on her belly where she could feel the baby's kick from time to time. The other hand was loosely clasped in Rajen's. There was a nip in the air but the sun was bright. Betty leaned back against the cushions and shut her eyes, a half-smile playing on her face. As Rajen looked on, still holding her hand, she began to hum softly. Soft and low, trying to remember half-forgotten folk songs, she paused in between, frowned as if trying to recall forgotten melodies, and then began again. The humming slowly grew into a song. From the musty attics of the mind the lyrics came back to her as she sang. In between, whatever lines she could not remember she hummed.

This is how the viceroy and his wife found them when their carriage laboured up the hill in an unannounced visit to their daughter. They saw Betty leaning back in the garden swing, with the Maharaja of Patiala bending over her. It was the kind of scene one would visualise in a dream: the idyllic backdrop, the newly-constructed palace, the garden full of flowers, and the pair of lovers on the swing lost in their own private world.

Hoping against hope, they had come one more time thinking they might persuade their daughter to return with them. But again, on seeing the couple together, they realised the futility of the thought and abandoned their plan. They spent a cheerful afternoon at the Chail Palace with them. Betty showed them the garden and the view from the upper levels of the palace. Her movements were slow, weighed down by the life growing within her, but she was thrilled about her new home and conveyed this enthusiasm to her parents through her excited chatter. After a round of the palace, Rajen offered to take the viceroy to see the cricket ground. They rode away on horseback while Betty and her mother stayed back. Happy to have some time to themselves, they talked about the coming big event. Betty told her mother how she looked forward to the baby. Her mother was apprehensive and persuaded her to return to Patiala for her confinement and take advantage of healthcare facilities there at Lady Dufferin Hospital and also the multi-specialty hospital that the maharaja was trying to set up. He had identified skilled doctors and physicians from different places and lured them to his state. In Chail there was little arrangement for obstetrics. Betty saw the logic in the argument and decided to talk to Rajen about returning to Patiala.

The sun had begun its downward descent and the chill was setting in when the viceroy and Rajen returned from their survey of the cricket ground. It was time for the viceroy and his wife to take leave of them. Betty and Rajen stood watching from the porch as their carriage rolled down the hill, Betty waving a lacey handkerchief to her parents until the coach disappeared round the bend. She was happy that the relationship between them was once again cordial. They had avoided all controversial topics on this visit: Her Majesty's annoyance, the British government's policy, or the ban imposed on the maharaja, preventing him from entering Simla again. This time the viceroy had come not as a government officer but as a father. Betty realised it and loved him for it.

BACK IN PATIALA

They returned to Patiala two months before the baby was due. Betty was most uncomfortable on the journey downhill. The covered carriage rolled and rattled. The baby inside was jolted and bumped. Betty was nauseous and her back hurt. Her feet were swollen and there were prominent varicose veins on her calves. Rajen preferred to ride back on his stallion but his progress was slow. In between he stopped several times to check on Betty. En route it began to rain. The monsoon season had begun and the roads were slushy. They had to halt on the way at a little village called Kalka and wait for a lull in the downpour before they could resume their journey. Although Betty was well propped up with pillows and cushions, even so, when they finally reached the plains she was relieved. The long, tiring journey finally over, the carriage with the accompanying horse-riders rolled into the royal city. Betty was weak and exhausted, almost fainting as she alighted from the carriage, clutching her belly. The servants of the palace, who were waiting to receive her, gathered her up and half-carried her into her chambers. The rajmata herself came down and gave appropriate instructions and sent for the gynaecologist from Lady Dufferin Hospital. Betty was attended to, fed, fussed over, and made to sleep off the fatigue. Rajen watched the scene helplessly, wishing he could be more useful to his young wife who was apparently in so much discomfort. Then, assured that she was well looked after, he left to attend to the affairs of the state which he had neglected all this while.

It was hot and humid in Patiala. Betty had a frail constitution made even frailer with the weight of pregnancy. In addition, the long journey from Chail had left her without much strength. In the days that followed she remained confined to her room and was looked after by her handmaids. Everyday the official doctor would look in and examine her. Although recovery was slow, the doctor reassured her that she would regain her strength within a few days. All she needed was good food, rest and care. She was getting enough of that so, in her opinion there was no need to worry. The varicose veins in her calves were painful but the doctor told her it was normal.

'Put your feet up, my dear, and rest. You will soon be well,' said the gynaecologist, an aged, white-haired, sari-clad woman who had served the royal family for the last three decades, presiding over the birth of every royal progeny in the palace.

Betty lay flat in bed, two fat pillows under her feet, her knitting needles always by her side, looking out through the window at the peepal tree in the garden. It was the same peepal tree she loved to watch from the Bryans' compound, only this time she was seeing it from the other side of the large ground, and from a different angle. The opposite side of the tree, not visible from the Bryans' garden, faced her window now. She saw the gnarled branches, the hollows in the trunk, and the squirrels chasing each other up and down. She saw a pair of owls sitting at the mouth of a large hollow in the eastern branch of the tree. They sat there silently, without moving, without making a sound, almost as though they were an inert part of the rough branch.

On the same side of the room, next to the window facing the garden was a door that opened onto a closed verandah. Twice a day Betty would emerge from her room and take a walk. Sometimes, in the morning when it was hot and humid, after Rajen left to attend to his duties, she would walk up and down in the verandah. And sometimes she would walk out into the garden and stroll along the flowerbeds, looking at the marigolds in bloom, the sunflowers and the zinnias. She would sit and feed the birds, watch them fight and peck each other for the crumbs she scattered along the pathway. The owls would look on silently as she walked up and down. They did not move but their eyes would follow her intently. Betty discovered with surprise that owls could actually turn their head right around to 180 degrees without moving at all. So it seemed as though they had eyes overlooking their backs. She also heard the low screech that owls emit. This was the sound she heard when a noisy eagle from above alighted on the higher branches of the peepal. The two owls made a low guttural sound and shuffled out of sight, into the hollow which was their home. On another occasion, early in the morning, she saw a peacock sitting on the parapet of the palace walls. Even as she watched in amazement, the mighty bird spread its wings and flew off into the woods beyond.

Betty observed all this and noted it in her diary. The long periods of rest with her feet up, the daily walks, the squirrels, the owls and the birds. All of them became a part of her long spidery jottings. Physically she had recouped; the swelling in her feet had subsided and her varicose veins were less painful. She wrote about the visits of the white-haired, sari-clad doctor who spent an hour with her every day. She wrote about Rajen who showed her the utmost consideration, spending all his free time by her side, fulfilling her slightest whims and fancies. Sometimes, much to the amusement of the other men in the palace, he even missed his evening polo to be by her side. They had not seen this tender side of the maharaja before.

Sometimes she got lonely and sent for Jasbir and Harbir. Their brother Attar Singh was still in Amritsar with his wife but there was still no truce with his in-laws. A child was on his way and perhaps the girl's parents would thaw when they saw their grandchild. So Betty was told. She felt a strange bond with the tall willowy girl she had seen only briefly by the side of the imposing young man and found herself thinking about her a lot, wondering how life was treating the young couple. Were they as happy as she was in her marital bliss and impending motherhood? Truly, there was little to dilute Betty's happiness. She was the favoured queen of the maharaja; the palace belonged to her; the people loved her; and now, any day she would hold a tiny bundle of joy in her arms. Was Attar's wife experiencing the same sense of fulfilment?

During those long, lazy days of waiting Betty remained cheerful and relaxed. The world was like one big incandescent stage lit up by a million rainbows. She was centre stage, getting love and care, applause and appreciation from all quarters. Sailing on cloud nine, she did not know that happiness was a bubble that could burst at any point of time. As she floated along merrily in her dream world, somewhere else another bubble was to burst first – suddenly, unexpectedly. It would burst without warning, destroying the fleeting moments of happiness that had come into the life of the tall, handsome, and noble Attar Singh.

It was still early one morning when Harbir came running into Betty's chamber without waiting for the maid to usher her in.

The maharaja was not around; he had gone to Kapurthala a day before for a meeting with his friend, Jagatjit Singh, the ruler of Kapurthala. Betty was still lingering in bed, half asleep. Harbir burst into the room shrieking loudly, sat down cross-legged with a thump on the floor by the large poster bed, and began beating her breasts. Astonished, Betty started up and asked her what the matter was. She had never seen Harbir behave this way. Nor had she ever seen such a blatant display of grief.

Harbir did not answer; she rocked to and fro and continued wailing. Her cries filled the entire wing of the palace and soon had the servants hurrying in to see what the matter was. They stopped at the doorway when they found their chhoti maharani sitting up in bed, staring helplessly at the girl beating her breast and careening on the floor. Someone ran to fetch a glass of water, another rushed to her side to quieten her. Betty looked on in consternation, not knowing what to do.

Gradually, Harbir's cries petered down to occasional sobs. She wiped her eyes and blew her nose noisily into her dupatta. Finally, composed enough to give voice to her sorrow, she narrated how they had received bad news from Amritsar just this morning. Her bhabi, Attar Singh's wife, who was well into the final stages of her pregnancy, had slipped and fallen from the stairs. She had hit her head against the banister and died before the doctor could be called in. The child in the womb had been taken out after a lengthy operation but was in a critical condition, being premature. The chances of the newborn baby boy's survival were slim but all efforts were being made. Jasbir had left for Amritsar along with her father. They would stand by Attar in his hour of need and pray for the baby's survival. Harbir had stayed behind to attend to their ailing mother.

The story came out in fits and starts, amid recurrent bouts of weeping and breast-beating, even as the maids of the household tried to calm her down. Betty was numb. Her fingers and toes had turned ice-cold and a chill ran down her spine. Her face was pale and wide-eyed, her hair dishevelled as she heard the sad story. Again and again her mind took her back to the scene on Baisakhi day in the compound of the gurudwara, when she had first met Attar and his new bride. And then the time when the couple was leaving for Amritsar and had come to say goodbye. How charming they looked side by side, what an elegant pair they made, and how happy they seemed. And now all that was over. Suddenly, inexplicably, joy was replaced by sorrow. And what about the child? Would he live or would he too follow his mother into the other world?

Betty felt a pain in the low abdomen as the baby inside turned over. She reminded herself that she should remain calm or else the unborn child would be agitated too. Taking deep breaths, she calmed herself before walking over to Harbir to pat her shoulder. She spoke to her soothingly, told her to calm down and pray that all would be well. The baby, Attar's prematurely delivered child, would pull through with the grace of the Gurus.

'Sit down here with me and let us all pray together,' said Betty.

A hush descended as the two of them sat down cross-legged on the carpet, covered their heads and began to pray. The servants hovering around too followed suit and joined them. '*Ek Onkar*' began as a low rhythmic chant and grew into a litany in which they all joined in. Eyes closed, palms joined in supplication, they all sang and prayed to the ten Gurus to spare the life of the newborn infant. Betty's chamber looked like the hall of a temple, full of devotees lost in prayer. As the sound of the *paath* echoed through the corridors and travelled to other parts of the palace, more people joined the congregation silently. Lost in prayer, they did not know when the rajmata entered the room and joined them. They did not even get to know when the badi maharani tiptoed down the corridor and stood awhile motionless at the doorway. Nobody saw her surveying the scene in silence; no one saw her gaze rest on Betty's serene face for a long while, those eyes shut in devotion, the veil over her head, her hands folded across her rounded belly. No one saw the cold dislike on the badi maharani's face as she quietly turned and walked away.

Prayers do not always go unheeded. They are sometimes answered by the powers that be. In the days that followed, news trickled in from Amritsar that the child had survived. He was a bonny little fellow, fair-complexioned and light-eyed like his mother. They named him Kartar Singh. The father, Attar Singh, completely broken after the sudden demise of his beloved wife, took solace in the fact that a part of her still lived on. Jasbir, the child's paternal aunt, offered to bring up the child. She would bring Kartar to Patiala where she and Harbir would both look after their nephew. Attar Singh did not protest. He knew he would not be able to take on the duties of a single parent, so he allowed the baby to be moved to Patiala, under the tender loving care of his paternal aunts, Harbir and Jasbir. This was the information given to the chhoti maharani one evening as she sat by her window, looking out at the great peepal tree in the garden, wondering where the owl family had disappeared. She had not seen any of the night birds for several days now.

The same evening, on 19 August 1893, Betty took out her little red diary and recorded the painful events of the day.

Attar's wife must have had a dream before her eyes. She must have visualised her son growing up into a sturdy handsome sardar, a soldier in the maharaja's army, a responsible young man with the world at his finger-tips. She must have dreamt some dreams of his future – the hopes, the aspirations, the ambitions. And she must have had some dreams of her own future with her loving husband Attar Singh.

Where are those dreams now? All gone, all blown away with the wind. With that single slip of the foot, the fall from the stairs, the pool of blood on the floor and those glassy eyes staring forevermore into empty space.

Yes, it disturbs me. I can feel my womb tighten against the tragic picture. I can feel that my unborn child is upset. But I must not think of it. I must control myself and not get agitated. Let my child continue growing inside me peacefully until the time comes for him to be born. Let me focus on happier matters.

But how do I get that beautiful dead woman out of my mind? She haunts me!

When Rajen walked into the room he found her holding her notebook close to her chest, her eyes tightly shut, a stray tear trickling down her cheek.

RAJKUMAR

MOTHERHOOD

The monsoon clouds were still hovering above the royal palace when Betty woke up the next morning in great pain. The maharaja heard her groaning and sent for his mother who, in turn called the doctor and the *dai*, the midwife who had been visiting Betty regularly. The chhoti maharani's chamber was swiftly converted into a mini-hospital with attendants brought in to assist the birth of a royal baby. This was no occasion for men to be around so the maharaja, although he was keen on sitting by his wife's bedside and holding her hand, was sent away by his mother to the office wing of the palace. The rajmata herself moved to a corner of the room, sat down cross-legged on the floor and began counting the beads in her rosary, muttering the *bani* under her breath. As the new life trapped inside Betty struggled to come into the world amid a painful labour, the attendants bustled around, trying to be helpful and the white-haired sari-clad doctor reassured everyone that everything was normal and there was no need to worry about the health of the child or the mother. The moans subsided for a while and then began again, more intense, more urgent. Once again there was a lull and Betty recovered her breath while a maid dabbed her moist brow. The pains returned with shorter intervals again until finally, in the midst of a prolonged, unabated, seemingly endless cry, the baby emerged and took his place in the mortal world. The palace acquired its new prince, second in line to succession after the badi maharani's son, the Yuvraj Bhupinder Singh.

As the new baby grew, Betty regained her strength gradually. She was well looked after. The rajmata was in and out of her chambers. On his mother's insistence, Rajen was persuaded to move to the adjoining rooms for the first forty days after the prince's birth. He was not happy with the proposal but this was the custom and so he bowed before it. The new mother needed time and space to overcome the ordeal of labour. He would cool his heels meanwhile and attend to other work of the state.

His heart, however, lingered on in the chhoti maharani's chamber where he would look in off and on, whenever he got the chance. Sometimes he would be sent away from the door as the new mother was either being bathed or massaged. On other occasions he was allowed to sit by her bedside and watch the baby being cleaned and sponged. He was a tiny creature with little brown fuzz on his head. His complexion was light – in fact, very pink in the first few days – and his eyes were blue, like his mother's. Rajen looked at the baby from a distance, not trusting himself to take him in his lap for he seemed too weak and vulnerable. Perhaps, when the child grew bigger he would overcome his fear, put him on his lap and play with him.

Motherhood suited Betty. Her face acquired a gentle expression, especially when she looked at the baby. Her mouth widened into a smile and a twinkle appeared in her eyes when she cooed and talked to the infant. Rajen would lean back in his chair by the bedside and watch her feed the child, the buttons of her loose kurta opened down to waist, her breast half covered with her dupatta. As the baby sucked, he would fall asleep and then Betty would shake him gently to awaken him. The feed over, she would hand him over to the waiting maid so that she would put him on her shoulder to burp. Fast asleep and contented, the baby would then be placed in his crib next to Betty's bed, close to the window. A net curtain would cover the crib to keep out mosquitoes and flies. A maid would stand in attendance all the time, swinging a *pakkha*, a hand-fan, to keep the baby cool. Occasionally the maid was given relief when Betty told her she could take a break, like she did now, when Rajen came in to visit her.

'What are we going to call him, my dear?' she asked, holding the child close.

'Well, we have to consult the *granthi*. He will give us an *akkhar*, a letter with which his name will begin. Then we will have a ceremony, a *naam-karan*, which will be a big state event,' Rajen told her.

This, too, was new for Betty who was familiar with sanitised christening ceremonies in the church where a baby was named after a parent or grandparent or godfather/godmother. But she accepted it the way she accepted all the new customs and rituals of the Sikh community. After all, when she decided to share Rajen's life she had a fair idea of what would be involved. This was just a part of the package deal and she had no regrets. She had been thinking of a name but could not decide on any single one. Perhaps the choice of a letter would make it easier.

When forty days were over, a grand function was held at the palace. Elaborate prayers were followed by a *langar* in which the entire population of the palace seemed to participate. 'R' was the letter the priests took out for the new baby, so they had to choose a name beginning with R.

'Can we call him Richard? After my great-uncle? He was Sir Richard Burton, knighted by Her Majesty,' said Betty hesitantly when they were back in their chambers. Betty was propped up against high pillows, the baby in her lap. Rajen sat on a chair by her side, observing the baby's movements closely, wondering if he would dare to pick him up now.

'Well,' he replied thoughtfully, 'you see, he has to be a "Singh" the way all of us, Sikhs, are. So Richard Singh would not really....' He left the sentence incomplete.

'I get it,' said Betty quickly. 'We will think of something else.'

Then after a moment she added: 'Perhaps we could keep it as a middle name? Or a prefix?'

'Yes, why not? Let's decide on the proper name first.'

There was a lull in their conversation. A lull punctuated by the cooing and gurgling sounds made by the baby. Rajen leaned forward and examined the baby's toes closely, each little toe complete with a pearly pink nail. The baby turned his blue eyes toward his father and continued cooing. His skin had changed colour; no longer pink, it was now more creamy white, like his mother's. Still tiny, he easily fitted between the crook of Rajen's arm and his open hand. The maharaja had finally picked up his son. Betty looked on and smiled.

'Ram Rahim,' said Rajen as he looked down at those trusting blue eyes.

'Huh?' Betty looked at him askance.

'We'll call him Ram Rahim. Sri Richard Ram Rahim Singh,' he said after a pause.

'Where did you get this name from?' she was curious.

'He is a Singh. He has English blood, so he can be Richard, too. But it would be inappropriate to call him 'Sir' so let him be 'Sri'. Sri Richard. And he is going to be on good terms with the Hindus and Muslims, so let him be Ram Rahim. In his name he will combine the secular and progressive spirit of our times. How are you, Sri Richard Ram Rahim Singh?' said Rajen and tickled his newly-named son under the chin. The baby cooed as if in response.

'He looks every bit an angrez, doesn't he?' asked Rajen.

'He does,' Betty agreed. 'But they say babies change their appearance every few weeks. So let us wait and see.'

'Sri Richard Ram Rahim Singh, you'd better grow up fast,' said Rajen in a lisp. 'For now I will simply call you Kaka. Kaka-ji, *tussi great ho*!'

Kaka-ji. That was the prince, the Rajkumar. That was his first name. Kaka *aka* Sri Richard Ram Rahim Singh, the name given to the prince by his parents, Betty and Rajen. It was a name that would soon be taken away from him, even before he learned to say it. This name, which he acquired when his father held him in his arms for the first time, would soon be abandoned. Kaka was to be christened all over again without anyone knowing it.

If this seems unusual, there was indeed a lot that was unusual in the pattern of events that followed.

The new prince was now two months old. His name was publicly announced. It was a name that was different, to say the least. When one heard it for the first time invariably the reaction was incredulity: 'Oh, really?' A raised eyebrow. Then amusement; then a shrug of the shoulders and an indulgent remark like 'it's probably one of the maharaja's whims,' followed by an acceptance of the strange-sounding name. Popularly known as Kaka-ji, he was the apple of everyone's eye, the blue-eyed prince of the younger maharani.

The weather changed after Diwali and there was a nip in the air. In the evenings, Betty would need a shawl as she strolled down the garden. A maid would wheel the baby stroller with the prince in it. Together they would walk down the aisle, past the Bryans' courtyard. Sometimes Betty would stop en route to chat with Minnie. Occasionally she would step in for a quick cup of tea. They would relive the few months spent together in the apartment when she had first come to Patiala with the maharaja.

Strange as it may seem, for the people of Patiala, Betty was still the daughter of Charles and Minnie Bryan. True, they accepted her as their queen, but they also believed that their queen was Miss Florence Bryan before she became Maharani Harnam Kaur. In any case, it did not bother them, so fully they had embraced her, and so disarmed were they with the warmth she exuded, her innocent beauty and the manner in which she had espoused the Sikh faith. In all probability, they would never have believed it if someone had told them that their queen was in fact the daughter of Her Majesty's regent, the viceroy. '*Maharani Harnam Kaur di jai*' was the slogan that greeted her whenever she came out in public. A new slogan now was '*Rajkumar Kaka ji di jai*' when they saw her with the prince.

She enjoyed the feeling of being in power, the sense of importance, and the fact that the public loved her. She enjoyed it as much as she enjoyed the winter sun, sitting in her verandah with her baby, scribbling happily in her diary, recording all the myriad experiences life had subjected her to. Somewhere high above was the intermittent song of a koel sitting on a branch of the peepal tree. A few feet from her chair were a dozen sparrows, chirping merrily. Betty seeped in all these sights and sounds, recording them in her notebook.

A BOLT FROM THE BLUE

As she sat writing, footsteps approached her and the maid said softly: 'Rani sahiba, your milk.'

'Leave it here,' replied Betty, not looking up from her diary.

The maid placed the glass of milk, covered with a saucer, on the table beside her and went away silently. On the doctor's advice, Betty had increased her intake of milk. Nursing mothers need extra nourishment, so she was told. Twice a day she would have a glass of milk. Invariably, in the mornings she would sit in the verandah and sip her milk slowly.

Today she reached out for the milk, found the glass too hot to touch, so she let it cool, without taking a sip. A few minutes later, as she continued to scribble in her diary, the baby whimpered in the crib inside. Putting down her diary, she went back into the room to Kaka's crib. He had soiled his nappy, so she called out to the nanny, asked her to change his diaper, and returned to the verandah. The glass of milk still stood on the table but sniffing it curiously was Misty, the Bryans' cat. Betty loved the feline creature and would often give it milk, the way she did today. Pouring some from her glass into a saucer, she placed it on the floor and called out to the cat.

'Come, Kitty, this is for you,' and pushed the plate towards the cat who stood watching her attentively.

Gradually the cat inched up to the saucer. She lapped up the milk, cleaning up the saucer with long sweeps of her tongue.

'Good Kitty,' muttered Betty softly, 'You were hungry, weren't you?'

But the cat paid no heed. Instead it growled noisily and began frothing at the mouth. As Betty watched, the cat doddered and fell prostrated before Betty's chair, overturning the glass of milk. It writhed and squirmed for a while, then stopped all movement. Misty the cat was dead.

Betty watched horrified. What was happening under her very nose? She could not quite figure out.

As she looked on thunderstruck, footsteps approached from behind and a voice said: 'Rani sahiba, your milk.'

Betty whirled around in terror: 'But you just gave it to me,' she pointed at the half-empty glass, 'and see what it did to the cat!'

The maid looked puzzled, 'No, Rani sahiba, I have just come from the kitchen. I am late because my *jutti* broke on the way and I had to go back to wear another pair.'

'Then who brought me the milk?' Betty asked.

'I don't know, Rani sahiba, it wasn't me.' She looked again at the glass and continued, 'and this is not one of our glasses. We do not have anything like this in our kitchen.'

Betty was trembling but she did not want to make a scene in the maid's presence so she sent her away. The maid seemed equally disturbed. As she bent to pick up the glass that was already there next to the dead cat, Betty admonished her, 'No, leave that alone. Don't touch it.'

Surprised, the maid withdrew. As she retreated, Betty hurriedly ran across to the Bryans' house to tell them what had happened to the cat.

Minnie was shocked. More than the loss of the cat, it was another disturbing thought that was beginning to take shape in her mind. She was lost in thought as she gathered up the dead cat which was now beginning to stiffen up.

'Don't you realise, my dear, the milk was meant for you!' she said finally in a low voice.

Suddenly it sank in and Betty turned cold. True, she was supposed to drink up the milk and die the way Misty did, writhing and squirming, frothing at the mouth. Someone clearly did not want her to live.

But who?

Minnie caught her just in time as Betty collapsed on the carpet.

Rajen was livid when the news reached him. Minnie had sent word to Charles Bryan who in turn informed the maharaja of what had taken place. Almost immediately, Rajen had returned to Betty's chamber. He found the lady doctor by her side, counting her pulse. The rajmata was also present, a grim look on her face. Betty herself was in a state of shock.

'She is fine now,' the wizened old doctor assured the maharaja before leaving. 'But you need to make better security arrangements.'

The rajmata took charge of the situation. All the servants who were present were called and she addressed them privately, sternly admonishing them to take greater care of the chhoti maharani. She also swore them to secrecy and warned them that news of what happened that morning should not go beyond the chamber walls. If this kind of information reached the gossip mills there would be no end to it; it would be fanned and distorted. Besides, whoever was making mischief would become extra cautious and would be hard to pin down. Investigations would be conducted and the guilty would be taken to task.

The maharaja privately entrusted Charles Bryan to carry out an investigation into the matter. Again, utmost secrecy was to be maintained for political reasons. Betty recovered and life went back to a semblance of normalcy. The only difference was that now Minnie personally attended on her needs, supervising the preparation of her meals and refreshments. She also kept a close eye on the little prince. Harbir and Jasbir, who were completely trustworthy, were both away to Amritsar and would return soon. Until then, Minnie would be solely in charge.

In the following month of December, Harbir and Jasbir returned from Amritsar, bringing with them the baby Kartar. They became surrogate mothers for their brother's son and devoted themselves entirely to his well-being. As the baby was very weak, having had a premature birth, the first winter was critical and he had to be protected from exposure. One of his aunts was constantly with him while the other attended to routine jobs. Gradually they started taking turns to visit Betty, so Minnie could now take time off in between her duties. By the time the Lohri festival came around, life was pretty much regulated, the Misty episode was almost forgotten, Betty had almost regained her girlish figure and Prince Kaka was learning to roll over onto his stomach.

No one ever found out who was responsible for Misty's death. The network of the maharaja's spies spread its tentacles through the palace and even in the city, but could gather no information. To all appearances, it was an insider's sleight of hand. Who was this insider and what were the motives? One could never be sure although there were speculations galore. Tight security was maintained to prevent any mishap.

ANOTHER LOHRI

During the weeks preceding Lohri, again the royal city of Patiala began donning a festive look. Once again there was the sound of drums, singing and dancing in the streets. Preparations for the royal celebration were afoot. After all, it was again a prince's first Lohri. Last time it was the badi maharani's firstborn, this time the chhoti maharani's. The new prince was the second in the line of succession; the occasion demanded an appropriate celebration, like last year's.

Once more there were gifts of clothes, jewels, sweets and dry fruit distributed among the people. Gift hampers were sent to the homes of all the maharaja's aides and alms were given in charity to beggars. The royal house was known for its benevolence and gained the goodwill of the masses all over again. Just as the badi maharani had received an expensive *naulakha haar* on the last Lohri, this time it was Betty's turn to get a similar gift from the rajmata.

It was on Lohri day that the maharaja's palace received two important visitors. One was the maharaja's sister, Bibi Bachtiar, who came with her children from Lahore. She had not yet seen Kaka and wished to attend his first Lohri. Her husband, Sardar Jivan Singh, was one of the prominent citizens of Lahore whose late father had helped the British forces in the 1857 crisis. In recognition of his father's services Jivan Singh was among the trusted Indians the British liked to associate with. He had recently been created a CSI, the Companion of the Most Exalted Order of the Star of India.

The other distinguished visitor was the maharaja's friend, Jagatjit Singh, ruler of Kapurthala. Like Rajen, Jagatjit had been a regular guest at the viceregal parties in Simla but now he too was banned from entering the summer capital of the British. Jagatjit had continued his bonhomie with Rajen in the Chail Palace. Now, on the occasion of Lohri, he decided to visit his friend in Patiala with gifts for his newborn son.

Sitting around the Lohri bonfire, Betty did not dance the way she had danced on the last Lohri celebration. She held Kaka, wrapped up carefully in a blanket, in her lap. When people approached her she smiled and responded to their greeting in an appropriate manner, but she did not once leave her seat. Nor did she hand over her baby to anyone but Jasbir. Harbir had stayed back with Kartar, who was slightly indisposed. Betty, who had not yet seen Kartar, asked how the baby was doing.

'Fine, Rani sahiba. He is growing well but tends to fall sick easily. That's why we did not bring him here,' his aunt replied.

'When he is strong enough, why don't you bring him over to see me?' asked Betty. 'He and Kaka could play together.'

The babies were still too young to play but Betty was dreaming of a not-too-distant future when two little boys would reach out for the same rattles and toys, crawl together and take their first doddering steps simultaneously.

'Yes, Rani sahiba, we will bring him to meet Kaka-ji. In fact, he seems to be just like Kaka. He's about the same size and the same complexion. Only the colour of his eyes is light-brown,' said the girl, looking into Kaka's blue-grey eyes.

The badi maharani did not attend the Lohri celebration. Rajmata had sent for her but she excused herself saying she was unwell. When the rajmata received her reply she raised an eyebrow but did not say anything. Next to her sat Bibi Bachtiar Kaur, her daughter from Lahore. Her children ran around the courtyard, singing and dancing with the professional singers. Rajen's sister, Bibi Bachtiar, was particularly affectionate towards Betty. She brought gifts from Lahore for her and Kaka. From time to time she turned to the baby and cooed at him.

'Come to bua, Kaka,' she cooed and Kaka seemed to understand because he gurgled in response and tried to reach out for her dangling earrings.

Betty allowed Rajen's sister to hold Kaka for a while and they continued to exchange pleasantries. Betty accepted the invitation to visit Lahore during the coming season whenever Rajen could organise a visit. They chatted pleasantly as the happy festive noises of the Lohri celebrations continued around them, the dancing, the singing and the merry-making.

A surprise hamper arrived for Kaka on Lohri day from the viceroy and his wife. It had travelled all the way from Calcutta. Among new clothes and accessories, it comprised some clothes, toys and baubles for Kaka, an exquisite diamond bracelet for Betty and bejewelled gold spurs for Rajen. Along with the hamper came a warmly-written note from the viceroy's wife, telling Betty how much she missed having her around and how she was eager to set eyes on her and the baby. Coming down to Patiala was not possible at that point but perhaps once they came back to Simla a meeting would be possible. In March the government machinery would be on the road again, heading for the summer capital. Once installed in the hill-station, they would be close to Betty again. Then they would easily ride up to Chail Palace, pay them a visit and see Kaka for the first time. Meanwhile, the vicereine exhorted Betty to take utmost care of herself and the baby.

Betty was pleased to hear from her mother, especially when she sensed the warmth of feelings conveyed in the note. She realised how much she had missed her lately, in fact ever since the Misty episode, she had repeatedly thought of her mother, wondering what she would do in her situation. How would she react? What would she advise? Perhaps they could have a serious discussion once they met in Chail. The older woman would give her some practical advice on how best to handle the situation. True, Minnie was with her all the time, and she was very good, very caring, but there was a point beyond which she could not get close to Minnie, just as there were certain unidentified boundary-lines between her and the sisters, Jasbir and Harbir. Betty looked forward to Chail again, but Chail was not as lively as Patiala and it could be lonely at times. So she had persuaded Jasbir and

Harbir to come along, bringing with them the baby Kartar. The change would do all of them good and she would have some company, too. Besides, ever since she had witnessed the agonised death of the Bryans' cat, Betty had been haunted by all sorts of nightmares and strange fears. She would wake up suddenly in the middle of the night and imagine someone standing at her window with an unsheathed sword. Or she would be unduly disturbed by the shadow of a swinging creeper on the curtain, the mewling of a cat, or the howling of a dog. Even the screech of an owl would now make her shiver with fright. No longer did she feel safe in Patiala. It was as though unseen eyes were watching her all the time. She felt Chail might be a safer place.

Early in March, there was still a chill in the morning breeze; the sun had not yet begun to inflict its ire on the world; Holi, the festival of colours, was two weeks away when Betty told the maharaja that she would like to move to the Chail Palace. Rajen agreed. Chail was his summer capital, just as Simla was for the Englishmen. If Simla was their Mount Olympus, he would show them that Chail was his Kailash Parvat, much higher than the Olympus, and with many more gods of the Indian pantheon. Last year they had to cut short their visit because Kaka was on his way but this time there would be no such urgency and they could stay on for a longer spell.

Before they left en masse for the hills, Attar Singh made a brief visit from Amritsar to see his son, Kartar. He spent the day with his parents and his sisters, his baby gurgling and playing on his knee. Then he handed the child back to his sisters with a heavy heart, telling them to take good care of the baby once they went to the hills. Bidding them goodbye, he went to meet the maharaja, swore his allegiance to the house of Patiala all over again, and returned to Amritsar. He did not know what fate had in store for him and his baby. He had no idea that this was the last time he would see his little Kartar alive.

TRAGEDY STRIKES THE CRADLE

Kaka and Kartar were by now beginning to crawl. Although there was a difference of two months between them, they seemed to be similar in size and appearance. In fact when they slept it was only with the help of the clothes they wore that the two could be distinguished. Even so, the clothes were also similar most of the time because Betty, in her generosity, would buy identical clothes for Kaka and for Kartar, the motherless boy. Both the babies were fair-complexioned, both had light brown hair and light eyes, with just a shade's difference. When they crawled on the floor together they were a delight to watch – like a pair of twins, almost identical. Harbir and Jasbir doted over the duo and were in constant attention, hovering about them.

When the maharaja was away on work during the day, invariably Harbir and Jasbir would spend time with Betty, helping her look after the little prince. Once Rajen returned after his afternoon game of cricket with his eleven, or from the polo grounds, they would make themselves scarce, showing up only when their help was called to give the prince his milk or to walk him in the garden.

One afternoon, about a fortnight before they were to leave for Chail Palace, Betty sat at her desk by the window, writing in her diary. The room in which she and Kaka spent most of their time was large and L-shaped. The windows overlooking the garden and the peepal tree invariably had the curtains drawn aside to let in the bright sunshine. Kaka's cot was close to one of the windows while Betty's desk, where she liked to sit and write in her diary, faced another. In between was the door leading to the private verandah from where she could walk out into the garden if she so wished. From the desk where she sat writing, entering the events of the week faithfully into her diary, the view of the extensive palace grounds was remarkable. She could also see the corner of the garden where the dahlias were still in bloom. The path leading to the palace from the polo grounds was also visible. As she sat writing, she looked up from her notebook and out of the window, lost in her thoughts. It was one of those lazy afternoons when the sun seemed to be suspended in the sky, uncertain whether it would rise or set. Not a shadow of a cloud could be seen in the blue skies above, nor was there the slightest movement of a single leaf in the peepal tree. Not a bird, not a squirrel, not an owl stirred to break the somnolence of the scene. As Betty looked on absent-mindedly, she could see the marigolds growing all along the curve of the aisle. All along the walkway ran flowerbeds with late winter flowers still in bloom; somewhere in the distance on the far side, a group of workers was trying to level a path across an uneven terrain leading from the cricket field. Closer to the palace, along the hedges bordering the aisle, she saw a shadow move stealthily. As she looked absent-mindedly, she did not register it at first. But then the shadow stopped behind a tall cyprus tree, looked around in all directions, and then started walking furtively again towards the palace building. It was a turbaned person wearing a long cloak and Betty could not figure out if it was a young man or old, or if he was a servant of the palace or one of the officers. Whoever it was, there was no denying that he knew what he was about, judging from the sure-footedness of his measured long strides.

She got up from her seat, walked around the desk and moved closer to the window but by then the shadow had disappeared, probably gone to the other side of the building. Nobody was to be seen within the vicinity of the palace. She felt a bit uneasy about the slinking figure edging close to the palace. But then she shrugged and told herself she was probably imagining non-existent fears and tried to put it out of her mind. The little prince played on the floor with Kartar; Jasbir was engaged in a squabble with her sister who had buttoned Kartar's sweater back to front. The sweater was taken off so that it could be worn properly but by then the baby began to cry. He refused to wear the sweater again, kicking and screaming. Betty was disturbed.

'Why is the baby crying, Jasbir?' she asked.

'Rani sahiba, he doesn't want to wear his sweater. He will catch a chill, there's still a nip in the air,' said Harbir, struggling with the child.

'Hush, just wrap him up for now in Kaka's blanket. When he is quiet you can make him wear the sweater again,' instructed Betty.

Kaka, meanwhile, was picked up by Jasbir who sauntered out of the room with him before he too began to cry. This would invariably happen: if one baby cried the other one, too, would start crying.

Betty picked up Kaka's red velvet blanket and handed it to Harbir who wrapped it around Kartar and held him close, but the baby continued to cry.

'Here, give him to me,' Betty said.

Harbir handed Kartar to her. Almost immediately the baby started playing with the large ruby dangling from Betty's neck and stopped crying. A minute later, he opened his mouth in a big yawn and shut his eyes.

'The poor child is sleepy and you were not letting him sleep,' Betty admonished Harbir.

'Oh, dear, I'd better get his milk before he goes off to sleep,' said Harbir and dashed off to the kitchen to get a bottle of warm milk for the child.

Betty stood holding Kartar for a while, then she put him down on Kaka's swinging cot. As she rocked the cot to and fro, singing softly, the baby relaxed and went off to sleep. Betty looked down, smiled and tucked him up in the blanket. As she turned away, she felt that she should cover the baby's head, too. So she looked around, saw Kaka's cap lying on the stool nearby and placed it on Kartar's head. The cap was a special one made for the prince. It had a jewel on the crest with a feather sticking out of it. When Kaka wore it he looked every bit a little prince, just as Kartar did now. Wrapped up in Kaka's shawl, with Kaka's royal woollen cap, Kartar too looked like a royal baby. In fact, now, with his eyes shut, no one could tell the difference.

But where was Kaka? As Betty turned and walked out of the room in search of Jasbir who had taken Kaka out, she saw Harbir returning and told her, 'Kartar is sleeping now, don't disturb him. You can give him his milk when he wakes up.'

'Yes, Rani sahiba,' Harbir placed the milk bottle on the table beside the baby's crib and said, 'Let me get Kaka-ji's milk before he too starts crying.'

They left the sleeping Kartar in the prince's cot; Harbir went to get milk from the kitchen and Betty went to get Kaka from his nursery across the corridor. She found Kaka playing with Jasbir; milk, evidently, was the last thing on his mind. He had just learned to blow bubbles and was busy blowing spit-bubbles into Jasbir's face.

'Hai *rabba*, how naughty he has become,' said Jasbir, wiping her face with her dupatta.

Kaka blew some more spittle into her face and she scolded him all over again.

The baby's face was covered with spittle; his collar as well as his sweater was damp with his spit-bubbles. His cheeks were puffed out, mouth rounded, face pink with exertion but he would not stop.

'My naughty child, what's all this?' scolded Betty.

He gurgled happily as he came to her. When she talked to him he was distracted and began pulling at the gold hoops dangling from her ears. Jasbir and Harbir fussed around him as usual, gave him his milk and took out a fresh set of clothes for him. Betty watched the whole exercise with an indulgent smile. Kaka was growing big and naughty. He was also outgrowing his clothes, she noted. Soon she would have to get him some more.

Cleaned and dried, they brought Kaka back from the nursery to Betty's room. His cot was still occupied by Kartar. As Betty walked across the room she noted that the window was wide open and the bottle of milk had fallen to the floor. The wind, perhaps, she thought. The baby would catch a cold: she went to close it. But there was no wind. The window, however, gaped wide. As she shut it, she turned to look at Kaka being brought in by the sisters. Jasbir and Harbir walked to the cot, Jasbir was carrying Kaka and Harbir quickly came forward to prepare his crib for him.

Then the entire scene seemed to freeze.

Harbir, bending over the cot, seemed to be transfixed. Jasbir, also bending over the cot to place Kaka in it, seemed to turn to stone. Betty, turning from the window, towards the cot, stopped motionless in her tracks. All three pairs of eyes stared aghast at the child who was lying inside the crib. Kartar, the baby, was certainly not sleeping. The royal cap that Betty had placed on his head was lying askew on the pillow. The blanket was half pulled off. His body was lying limp across the cot, arms and legs akimbo, palms wide open, unseeing eyes staring into nothingness. His mouth was a gaping hole caught in a silent scream and the lips were beginning to turn blue at the corners. There was no doubt about it – baby Kartar was dead, as dead could be.

They stood petrified for what seemed an eternity. They opened their mouths to scream but no sound came. The three young women almost simultaneously sank to the floor wordlessly, one of them with a happily gurgling baby in her lap, another clutching at the railing of a crib that housed a dead child, a third whose knees buckled under her at the realisation that the death that had struck so suddenly and viciously was actually meant for her child; that the baby that lay inert like a discarded rag-doll could have easily been hers.

This is how the maharaja found them when he returned from his game of polo at sundown: like nine pins, strewn on the floor of the chamber he shared with his beloved wife and child. The women, like fallen statues, soundless and motionless. A baby dead in the crib, like a rag-doll tossed aside.

He roared. The maharaja roared when he saw the rag-doll in the crib. The roar shook the three young women out of their trance. He roared a third time and life seemed to return to Betty who held out both arms toward him, as if for help. The two companions, Harbir and Jasbir, quickly rose from the floor, Jasbir holding the still laughing and cooing Kaka, Harbir, the limp body of Kartar.

And then the maharaja, seeing Kaka, snatched him from Jasbir's arms and examined him carefully before turning to Kartar. Colour drained from his face when he saw the child's limp body.

'What's all this?' he asked, shaken, holding Kaka in the crook of his right arm, helping Betty to her feet with the other. He helped her to a chair just as she collapsed again.

Harbir and Jasbir placed Kartar's body on the floor between them, covered him with his baby-sheet and began to cry soundlessly into their dupattas.

The death of a child is always hard to take. One moment you have a smiling, cooing, gurgling baby, the next moment he is nothing but an inert mass. He leaves behind empty spaces, hollows which were earlier filled with his laughter, clothes which are orphaned forevermore, toys which have lost their rightful owner, promises of a future belied and a thousand million regrets and unfulfilled dreams of what might have been. So was it in the case of Kartar. In the brief lifespan that was writ for him he had come into the world with a mixed bag of happiness and sorrow, of ups and downs, highs and lows. His was a closed chapter now.

Kartar's story was over.

Not really, though. Kartar was dead but his story was to continue. Jasbir and Harbir went back to their lodgings that evening with Kartar in their arms. The maharaja's palace had its windows closed shut and was plunged in darkness for the next few days as a mark of sorrow. Men and women dressed in sombre white clothes silently filed in and out of the visitor's lounge of the royal palace and paid condolence to the rajmata and the maharaja. Betty did not see them; it was given out that she was taken ill. It was given out that Betty's son, Kaka, the little prince Sri Richard Ram Rahim Singh, who was known as Kaka-ji, was suddenly taken ill and had died.

No one was told the true story – that it was Kartar who had died and not Kaka. No one was told of the foul-smelling swab of cotton wool that was found in Kartar's mouth. That had probably caused his death, that little ball of cotton wool soaked in something lethal, shoved into the mouth of the sleeping child. No one was told of how the maharaja, with the rajmata, the Bryans, and Attar's sisters, had gone into a huddle on the discovery of the dead child; realising the gravity of the situation and the fact that the innocent baby had lost his life because he was mistaken for the prince, they had decided on a swift course of action. Kaka, the prince, would take the place of Kartar and be sent away to safety with Jasbir and Harbir. However, it would be given out that the prince Kaka-ji had suddenly died. Jasbir and Harbir would leave for Chail the very next day with Kaka-ji. The word would be spread that they had gone to Amritsar so that Attar Singh could spend some time with his baby. For the sake of the personal safety of the prince, misleading announcements would be made for public consumption. In two weeks' time, as planned, Betty would also leave for Chail and be reunited with her baby.

These decisions were made by the maharaja and his mother in split seconds and events took place at such a lightning pace that Betty could barely understand what was going on. The sight of Kartar's dead body had left her dazed and shaken. It was as though she was in a stupor, half awake and half asleep. She had vaguely been aware of the hushed urgency of the conversation around her but could not comprehend what was happening. It was only when the maharaja briefed Jasbir and Harbir and they quickly came forward to take the prince away that she was shaken out of her trance.

'Where are you taking him?' she screamed when they tearfully picked him up and turned to go, leaving behind what was left of their own little protégé with the rajmata.

The maharaja held Betty back and spoke reassuringly, 'It's all for the best, my dear. I will explain.'

She tried to break free but his grip was strong and held her tight. The rajmata stood looking on with a stony face. Evidently, she too was in agreement with Rajen. Realising the futility of resisting, Betty sank into a chair and buried her face in her palms. Jasbir and Harbir left Kartar behind and took away Kaka, the little prince Richard Ram Rahim Singh. Then the maharaja advised Betty to take some rest and left her alone. The rajmata covered Kartar's body with a white sheet and instructed a servant to take it away to the parlour.

As for Betty, left alone in her chamber, she wondered what she should now do. Suddenly life seemed to be emptied of all meaning. True, she was still the queen of the palace and her son was second in line of succession to the throne after his father the maharaja and his stepbrother, the Yuvraj Bhupinder. Nothing could change that. But, whether she was responsible or not, someone else's baby had lost his life, her own Kaka had been wrenched away from her and she would now spend her time in grief until she held him in her arms again. She had an inexplicable sense of insecurity. Where would they take Kaka? Suppose something were to happen to him? She sat by the empty crib, rocking it aimlessly. The sadness in her heart was overwhelming. It rose steadily, like the sea at high tide. She felt herself being sucked into its waters, deeper and deeper. Now it was up to her chest, constricting her heart. It rose further and caught her by the neck. The lump in the throat was hard to swallow. It gradually loosened and overflowed through her tear ducts. Rivers of grief ran down her cheeks. Her shoulders shook silently with sobs that she tried to control. She felt her world crumble around her.

And then a strong hand shook her by the shoulder. She shuddered with fright but it was just the maharaja, looking down at her grim and concerned.

'Just a few days, my dear, and you will be with your child again,' he told her softly.

He stroked her head gently as she buried her face in his chest and wept.

Following the orders of the maharaja and the rajmata, Jasbir and Harbir were not given time to mourn over their nephew. Their parents were not allowed to see their grandson for the last time. Attar Singh was not allowed to come to Patiala to see his little boy given state honours and cremated. It was a funeral worthy of a prince. No one knew that the little body wrapped in white for whom such elaborate rites were conducted was not the prince's. No one got wind of the fact that in the wee hours of the morning after the tragedy had taken place, Harbir and Jasbir had left Patiala in a closed carriage for Amritsar. There they would remain for the next two weeks. Kaka would be installed in Attar Singh's world in Amritsar as his child, born to the woman who had died in childbirth the year before, being brought up by his paternal aunts.

Attar Singh and his sisters, though broken-hearted at the loss of the baby Kartar, understood the royal reasons for this kind of public deception. The Patiala palace had always been a hotbed of intrigue and conspiracy but their family had been loyal servants of the kings in power. Their loyalty to the throne, the ruler and his interests was unequivocal. They would defend the interests of the state with their last breath. It was unthinkable for them to question the dictates of the maharaja. So, without hesitation, they complied with the maharaja's will, forgot their personal sorrow in the face of the imminent danger faced by the prince. Kaka would remain with them as long as the maharaja wished. He would take the place of Attar's son, Kartar, and be treated as such. The camouflage would be maintained for as long as the maharaja desired, or as long as the prince's life was in danger. They understood that now they had an urgent responsibility on their shoulders, a very important role to play as the custodians of a baby prince who would be second in line for the throne after his father. Realising the onerous task they had been entrusted with, Attar and his sisters would not be found wanting; they rose to the occasion and fervently pledged their loyalty to the maharaja all over again.

In the days that followed almost every day there was some missive or another from the maharaja, either asking about the baby's health or giving instructions pertaining to his safety. Further, Attar Singh was told that in two weeks' time the baby, along with Jasbir and Harbir, should be sent to Chail where they would spend the rest of the summer with the chhoti maharani. Jasbir and Harbir looked forward to their Chail trip. They had not travelled much. In fact, all they had seen beyond Patiala was the Amritsar district and, on one occasion, a bit of Lahore. They began making preparations for the long journey.

Rajen and his officers also busied themselves making preparations for the move to their summer capital. Rajen was determined to outdo the British in everything they did, so he made sure that his Chail Palace would have whatever Simla offered to the English populace, and even more. Yes, there would be parties, he told Betty. And balls and dances, whatever she was used to in the Viceregal Lodge. They would have distinguished guests, Indian royalty, and some select British officers – the viceroy, the governor and the chief commander.

'Let them impose a ban on my entry into their haven!' said Rajen defiantly. 'I will show them I do not need them. In fact they will be grovelling for my invitations. My abode is higher and better than theirs. I will look down at them from a higher seat.'

He had already invited the Maharaja of Kapurthala to visit him in Chail. Together they would hold festivities that would resound across the hills; the sounds would travel to the Englishmen's hilltop many miles away and make them go green with envy.

The long procession of carts and horses and buggies began its way towards the hill resort in exactly the same way as the British army trundled uphill to Simla, moving up slowly but steadily, stopping en route either for a change of horses or for a respite and meals. The chariot in which Betty travelled was a carriage for four. Along with her it also carried Jasbir and Harbir with their protégé. Minnie had almost decided to stay back in Patiala another week because Charles had to see to some last minute arrangements regarding the shifting of the official machinery. However, at the last minute, she too decided to accompany them and so the four women and baby found themselves in the closed carriage embarked on a long journey uphill. The road was long, but they were comfortable with each other and had the baby with them for amusement. Happily they allowed themselves to be carted up northwards.

Betty had been carefully instructed by the maharaja and his mother that she should not display any emotion on seeing Kaka again. It was part of the exercise to ensure his safety, so she was made to understand. Although it was hard to practise restraint, she did her best. Only when they were in the privacy of the closed carriage did she let her self-control go and grabbed the baby from his caretakers. For the rest of the long ride uphill she kept him in her lap, held him close, and baby-talked with him endlessly.

HIGHER THAN OLYMPUS

Summer on the Chail hilltop began on a peaceful note. The mountains seemed to have this calming effect, radiating peace and soothing nerves. The very air that Betty inhaled seemed to promote tranquility. At least this is how she felt once they were safely stationed in their palatial home overlooking the little mountain hamlet. The fears that had haunted her seemed to melt away and she could relax once again. The threats and shadows that were closing in around her in Patiala were left behind. She became carefree and happy once again and began to enjoy the company of her baby, spending happy carefree hours with him and the other women around her. It was, indeed, a memorable summer.

With the onset of autumn the hills began to change colour. From a deep green the leaves became a pale yellow. A yellow haze of pollen was in the air and it settled all over the lawns, the bushes, the garden and the path leading up to the palace. The viceroy's tenure in India had come to an end; he and his wife were preparing to return to London. Before leaving they made one final bid to persuade Betty to go along with them but with no success. For Betty life in Chail was nothing short of idyllic. She would not hear of leaving the place. The viceroy and his wife, realising the futility of trying to persuade her, sighed in resignation, packed their bags and left for England in the October of 1894. However, before leaving they promised Betty that they would be back the following summer, hoping that by then she would change her mind and return with them. They headed back to England soon after handing over charge to Lord Elgin, who took over as the new viceroy of India.

Betty missed her parents but lost in her little edenic world, she was soon distracted and life went on like before, the daily routine dominated by fun and games with the little prince.

This idyllic state of affairs was to last for another year and more. With the onset of the winter of 1894, Betty did not go back to Patiala. She stayed on with the baby and her companions, Jasbir and Harbir, who were now the constant buddies of Kaka, or Kunwar Kartar as he was known, the son of Sardar Attar Singh of Amritsar. When it snowed outside, together they would sit by the fireside and knit little woollen booties or sing songs. The maharaja occasionally shuttled between Patiala and Chail but Betty and her retinue remained in the Chail Palace through the difficult winter months. Then the spring came once more, the snows melted and the trees turned green again. Sad-eyed monkeys made their appearance once more on the cedar trees and dahlias sprang up overnight, growing wild on the mountain side. The little prince was beginning to talk nineteen to the dozen when Betty decided it was high time he began formal classes. The task of educating him was entrusted to Jasbir, who fixed a regular class schedule for Kaka.

Another summer on the hilltop came and went uneventfully.

Sometime towards the beginning of September of 1895, when they had been in their secluded haven on the mountain top for more than a year and a half, when the monsoons had receded and the air was beginning to acquire a delicious sharp edge, when the monkeys decided to move down to the lower reaches of the hills, and the green cover of the hills began to take on maturer autumn hues, an event long delayed was expected to take place finally: news came that the Bryans' daughter, Florence, had recovered from her protracted illness and was actually travelling to India. She would join them in Chail, for that was where Minnie lived most of the time with Betty's entourage. Initially the Bryans had been in a quandary, undecided how to tackle the issue.

After all, in the eyes of the public, the chhoti maharani was Florence, their daughter. So how could they now explain the appearance of another daughter called Florence?

They discussed the issue with the rajmata, who was briefly visiting the Chail Palace, and also with the maharaja but neither seemed too worried about it.

'You don't have to explain that you have another daughter,' was the nonchalant reply of the maharaja. 'And you could always think of another name.'

The rajmata was equally unperturbed about it: 'My younger daughter-in-law is Harnam Kaur. She is part of my family now and so she will remain. If you have another daughter visiting you, why should it affect anyone? They will get used to her just the way they got used to Harnam Kaur.'

She too suggested that it would be convenient to call her by another name. That would not be difficult, thought the Bryans, because their daughter was also known by her middle name, Gertrude, so calling her Gertie and introducing her as such would not be difficult. Barring the rajmata and the maharaja, no one knew that Betty was not Florence, their daughter, and so it would remain. The secret was to be maintained. The real Florence would, on arrival, be installed as their older daughter. However, the groundwork had to be prepared first and nothing could be taken for granted. Florence would have to understand the situation properly, get used to it, and then cooperate with them in keeping up the façade. As luck would have it, and as Minnie had stated on the first day that she set her eyes on Betty, both Florence and Betty were about the same height and build. Both had fair complexion and light eyes. Passing them off as sisters would not be difficult.

A week later, the real Miss Florence Bryan arrived in India. Even before she could enter the royal city of Patiala, she was met en route by her parents and taken to the Chail Palace. On the way the complexities of the situation were explained to her. She found the story strange and could not quite figure out why they were doing it, but because her father was in the maharaja's service and because the maharaja wanted it this way, Florence too complied. She did not mind being called Gertie and she certainly did not mind being treated as the junior queen's sister and the maharaja's sister-in-law. In fact she found the idea quite intriguing and was already thinking of the stories she would narrate once she got back home.

She had no inkling that she had left 'home' behind for good and was not destined to set foot on the English soil again.

Betty and Florence, who was now called Gertie, got along like a house on fire right from the day they first met. It was as though they had known each other for a long, long time. For Betty it was like being in touch with her childhood again. The first afternoon they met, the two of them sat on the swing in the garden outside the Chail Palace under the huge cedar tree, singing old folk songs remembered from kindergarten days. That was the beginning of a warm and easy relationship between the two.

Gertie's constitution, however, was not too strong and she had to protect herself from the mountain chill. When she sat outside for too long her nose would start running; if she took a walk in the garden she invariably came back sneezing; and if she left the windows open she would wake up with a headache. It was not easy for Gertie, as Betty could see. All the same, huddled in woollen shawls, sitting by the fireplace, they enjoyed each other's company, the peaceful ambience of the mountain top, the crisp mountain air, the view from the terrace, the warmth of the fireside and the numberless nursery songs they sang for little Kaka through the long evenings. Rajen would join them occasionally, riding up from Patiala, but most of the time the women of the palace were by themselves. Theirs was a closed world that no hostile element could infiltrate into. Here Betty felt that she and her child were safe once more. Gertie's health improved gradually and she began enjoying the cold, pristine beauty of the hills, the camaraderie and the hospitality of the palace.

Little did they know that the clock was ticking away and their time was running out. Even as the season changed, the wheels of fortune also turned; as winter gave way to spring and the snows melted again, their world too was to be transformed. Unrecognisable and irrevocably. Forevermore.

BEHIND THE SCENES

Unknown to Betty, there was a lot happening around her. While she was lost in a sort of delirium, spending time with Kaka, giving full play to her maternal instincts, she did not know that the maharaja and the new viceroy had been in serious communication. Betty was neither seasoned in the art of international politics, nor did she have much knowledge of the twists and turns of state governance. Her father, the former viceroy, was aware of her ignorance in matters of the state, as was her husband, the maharaja. Certain issues were simply beyond her ken so she was kept out of the picture while a major political move was being planned. Although she was at the focal point of the plans, she was kept in the dark. They knew that Betty, being hot-headed and headstrong, would never agree to their proposal. The maharaja too was well aware of this fact and was torn between his love for his wife and his duty as a politician-statesman. It was not easy for him to side with the dictates of the British Empire in a conspiracy of sorts against the woman he loved the most; for a long time, over many weeks, he refused to cooperate with the proposal Her Majesty sent through her regent, the viceroy. Initially he had rejected it outright. It was absurd, he expostulated. But the British statesman knew how to break his opponent's resolve slowly but surely. He did not give up: exercising the utmost patience, he withdrew pressure on the maharaja for a while and then, after a couple of weeks, when the ruler of Patiala was beginning to lower his defenses, the viceroy tried coercing him again on a more aggressive note. Again, after a few rounds of *in camera* conversation, the maharaja dug his heels in and again the viceroy stepped back but only for a while.

The tussle, the discussion, the arguments for and against carried on for about two or three months with British diplomacy trying its level best to break down the maharaja's iron will and the latter refusing to budge even an inch. Briefly, the bone of contention was Betty: Her Majesty had not taken her marriage to the maharaja in a kindly light and had repeatedly asked the viceroy to get his predecessor's daughter back from the Patiala stronghold. Betty's parents, too, had wanted to do the same before their return to England but they were reluctant to cause their daughter any unhappiness for there was no doubt that she was very happy being the wife of the maharaja of Patiala. Still, they had strong doubts: how long would she remain happy? After all, there had been attempts on her life;

her son had been attacked too and had fortunately escaped – but only to live incognito now lest he should lose his life. Moreover, looking closely at the history of the Patiala royal house, it was clear to the viceregal couple that polygamy was the accepted way of life for their maharajas. At that particular point of time the maharaja may be head over heels in love with their daughter, Betty, but who could predict the future? It was more than remotely possible that the young and virile ruler would soon tire of his new queen and start looking elsewhere for some more excitement and adventure.

All these doubts, however, were exchanged in privacy between the former viceroy and the vicereine. After their return to England these issues were still valid: they invariably found their way into the discussions held between the two powers – the English regent and the royal house of Patiala. The new viceroy was given strict and precise instructions by Her Majesty. When the talks led to no positive results then Lady Emily, Betty's mother, was sent back from England to India with the specific task of rescuing, by hook or by crook, her daughter from the clutches of the ruler of a vassal state. As it was Her Majesty's command it had to be followed. So now, in the early spring of 1896, Lady Emily had returned to Simla unannounced. She was again put up in the Viceregal Lodge from where she made a couple of visits to the Chail Palace to see her daughter. She did not discuss her mission with her, knowing full well what her daughter's reaction would be. She would patiently wait for the right moment. Meanwhile, she and the present viceroy, Lord Elgin, called the maharaja over for several serious discussions on the matter.

The rajmata joined in the discussions, too. In her chequered lifespan she had weathered good times and bad, had taken much in her stride, and was more knowledgeable in the ways of the world, far maturer than her son. Although she had never had the opportunity to rule the state, long years of experience had made her an astute politician and she could very well and very accurately predict the outcome of a wrong step taken. Not surprisingly, hers was the guiding hand behind all major political decisions. Ever since Betty had entered the palace, she knew that one day they would probably have to take a firm and unpleasant decision and send her back. Not that she had anything against her younger daughter-in-law; in fact she was rather fond of the girl and appreciated the manner in which she had tried to adjust to the Punjabi culture. However, she knew that Betty's life would always be in peril and so would her child's. Even though the common people of Patiala loved and respected her, the rajmata was aware of the lurking danger which could raise its ugly head at any time – the way it did when Misty, the cat died, or when baby Kartar was erroneously snuffed out, mistaken for the little prince. Much as she loved Betty and little Kaka, the rajmata knew that finally the time had come for the inevitable decision to be taken. She now entered the fray and sat at the meetings of the maharaja with the viceroy and Her Majesty's emissaries. The final decision they arrived at was after long, hard and heart-rending talks: Betty would go back with her parents to England. Rajen would not let Kaka go and fought hard to retain his custody. However, there was a general consensus that Patiala was too dangerous a place for the child. In fact the child's proximity to his father would spell his doom. Ultimately it was decided that the prince would stay on with his bua, his paternal aunt in Lahore. For his own safety, his identity as the prince of

Patiala and the grandson of the viceroy would never ever be revealed.

These crucial meetings were also attended by two other individuals who were to play a significant role in arriving at the final decision. One was Sardar Jivan Singh of Lahore who was married to Maharaja Rajinder Singh's sister, Bachtiar. The other was Maharaja Jagatjit Singh of Kapurthala. Both of them had maintained close ties with the maharaja; they weighed the pros and cons, considered the issue sympathetically and rose to the occasion. In fact, they personally offered to shoulder the responsibility of Kaka's upbringing and education. To all appearances, the baby would continue to be Attar Singh's son but Attar Singh, being a widower, would find it difficult to bring up the child, so the responsibility would be shared by the others: Jivan Singh and Jagatjit Singh would be his guardians. As the prince's life was fraught with danger in Patiala, he could live in the royal palace of Kapurthala if need be, or in the district of Lahore with his paternal aunt where he would be looked after in a manner befitting royalty and be well provided for.

At first the maharaja lost his cool, ranted and raved against the decisions taken. He was averse to the idea of being treated like a puppet and the fact that someone else should be making decisions and holding the strings of his personal life. However, he soon realised that he was up alone against the others at the table and lapsed into a gloomy silence. The viceroy and his predecessor's wife – Betty's mother – were determined that this time on no account would the latter leave her daughter behind to be targeted by some insane political assassin. The rajmata reasoned with her son; so did the maharaja's friend, Jagatjit, and his brother-in-law, Jivan

Singh. Attar Singh was called to attend one of the meetings and he, too, in his grave, respectful manner, endorsed the opinion of the majority. Finally, by the end of the discussions, the maharaja realised the futility of insisting on having his own way. He bowed before the collective wisdom of his well-wishers and put his signature on the document prepared carefully by the viceroy.

In brief, the document proposed by Her Majesty's regent and signed by the maharaja comprised the following clauses: first, that Betty would leave Patiala and go back with her parents to their Bowood Estate in England; second, that her child would not be told the secret of his parentage – he would grow up believing himself to be Attar Singh's son by his first wife who died in childbirth; three, that the child would be brought up as a conservative Sikh – he would never shave his beard or cut his hair; and finally, he would never own a passport, never leave the Indian border to go abroad, never try and seek his biological mother, even if he discovered the truth of his lineage. As the clauses were being read, Rajen sat at the table clutching his forehead. Nothing made sense to him any longer. All right, they wanted Betty back. The thought hurt like hell but everyone seemed to be convinced that it was not only expedient but also inevitable in the given circumstances; if he loved his wife he would have to let her go to a safety zone. Perhaps at a later stage, when her personal security was not in danger, she would find it safe to return to Patiala.

Privately, however, the vicereine knew they would never let it happen: once Betty came with her to England, the family was sure they would not let her go again. Back in London she would meet her old friends, learn to adjust to her own world once more, erase the past and forget the few years she spent as the junior queen of Patiala. But, would she forget the child she had given birth to? Well, collectively they would have to brainwash her into believing that in the child's interest she should stay away from him. Initially they would tell her that her separation from the child was only temporary and that he would join her in England as soon as Her Majesty gave her permission. This would buy them some time and perhaps they would come up with a better strategy in the meantime. Regarding the clause about the child growing up as a Sikh, they had considered the matter gravely. Kaka, now known as Kartar, had the fair complexion and blue eyes of his mother. His appearance was very English. However, if he grew up as a Sikh, with a beard and turban, his English features would be hidden under all the hair and no one would recognise him as an English woman's child. The final clause, the injunction that he was never to own a passport or leave the borders of India, was also deliberately included because the last thing that Betty's parents, particularly her mother, wanted was that the child should come looking for his mother in England. It was very clear to them that the child should stay with his own people in India. Kaka was a lovely baby but he belonged to a politically charged world; there were too many ifs and buts attached to his existence, far too many complications for the viceroy's family to be comfortable with. Tagging him along to England with Betty would simply be asking for more and more trouble. It would be best to leave him behind, take back their daughter, and begin afresh, making a complete break with the chaos that was India.

The agreement was signed and approved by the representatives of Her Majesty, the Queen of England. Rajen kept the secret in his heavy heart, not sharing it with Betty. He immersed himself more and more in his work, moving up and down from the hills to the plains almost every week. While in Chail he was withdrawn and gloomy even as he watched Betty play with the prince. He would ride off to the cricket field with his men and spend long hours on the pitch, trying to ignore the shadows closing in on him – the gathering gloom of his imminent parting with his beloved. Missives kept coming in from the Viceregal Lodge in Simla, goading him into action, but he kept dilly-dallying, postponing the eventuality. He did not know how to tell Betty that it was imperative for her to return to England with her mother. He looked for an appropriate occasion to break the news. He felt the time was not yet ripe and waited for the right moment when an opportunity would arrive and he would muster enough courage to tell the woman he loved that she must leave him.

It was in the spring season of the following year, 1896, when such an opportunity arrived, camouflaged under yet another tragic event.

The maharaja was in Patiala that week, attending a meeting with the rulers of the neighbouring states. Representatives from Nabha, Jind, Deegh, Malout, Amritsar, and Lahore had come down to Patiala to debate on the best way to battle the growing unrest among the masses. The monsoon had failed again and consequently, the agricultural produce had suffered, leading to greater poverty and misery among the common people. There was shortage of food and basic essentials. The outbreak of a famine seemed imminent; some solution was needed urgently.

Jivan Singh, the maharaja's brother-in-law, was present at the meeting, so was Attar Singh from Amritsar. The maharaja of Kapurthala sent his representative with a proposal that the waters of the five rivers of Punjab should be channelised so that all parts of the northern region would get enough water to irrigate their fields. This would, at least, stall famine in the coming season.

While they were in the midst of a serious discussion, a messenger arrived from the Chail Palace and delivered a sealed note to the maharaja. Adjourning the meeting, he withdrew to his private room to read its contents.

No one ever got to know what the letter contained but almost immediately he stormed out, brows knitted, face flushed, and shouted for his horse to be brought to him. Within a matter of minutes the maharaja, accompanied by Attar Singh, Jivan Singh, Charles Bryan, and a couple of horsemen, left for Chail: half a dozen horses leaving a dusty trail behind them as they galloped away across the plains and towards the hills.

ANOTHER CALAMITY

Charles and Minnie Bryans' daughter, who was visiting from England, was dead. She was found dead one early morning when the maid knocked at her door with her tea tray. No one knew how and why. She and Betty had chatted late into the previous night, sitting by the fireplace. Betty had then gone up to her room and Gertie must have followed some time later. What happened in the interim no one knew. Minnie Bryan, her mother sleeping in the adjoining room, was an early riser and had gone for a morning walk into the garden as usual. On this particular day she headed further down the hill, looking for a particular kind of hill mushroom that she would cook for breakfast. It was an old Irish recipe that she wanted to try out again: omelette stuffed with herbs and mushrooms. Her daughter would perhaps enjoy it. As she walked on further, Minnie lost track of time. She found some mushrooms, some coriander growing wild on the hillside, and also some nasturtiums and salvias, flowers that were not only edible but also added colour to the meal being served. Minnie gathered them up in a little basket and turned back, climbing up the hill again towards the palace.

As she entered the building, a strange hush greeted her. The usual early-morning hustle-bustle about the hallway was missing. She called out to the maids but no one answered. Even the doorkeeper on duty was nowhere to be seen. Minnie climbed up the stairs, turned left towards the maharani's chamber and found the door ajar. On the opposite side of the corridor, the rajmata's room was also wide open. Tracing her steps back, she walked towards her room on the other end of the corridor; as she approached, she heard a low hum of voices coming from her daughter's room. The door was open and everyone seemed to be gathered there – the rajmata, her daughter, Bibi Bachtiar from Lahore, Betty, Jasbir and Harbir. A couple of servants stood around silently watching. Gertie lay in bed, stiff and wide-eyed. There was no doubt about it – she was dead. Very dead.

One more unexplained, unnatural death. Once again a sudden bolt from the blue. Once again the façade of peace and tranquility had been shattered. How did she die? Was it a natural death or a murder? What was the motive? Who were the killers? Did they access the room through the window that had been forced open? So many questions unasked, unanswered. Unanswerable. Once again the air was fraught with danger. Once more there was death lurking at every corner, waiting to strike the unprepared. Adding more serious overtones to the event was the fact that until recently this particular room was being used by the chhoti maharani because her regular room was being given a fresh coat of paint. Just a few days earlier Betty had moved back into her own room. So was it again a case of mistaken identity? And was the intended target Betty? Did this mean that there were hidden enemies lurking about even in the midst of this paradise on the hilltop?

Once again the rajmata took charge of the situation. Sealed envelopes were sent immediately to the maharaja in Patiala and the viceroy in Simla. The viceroy's carriage rolled up within a few hours and out tumbled his aide along with Betty's mother. They were hurriedly ushered into an inner parlour where Betty, close to hysteria, holding Kaka tight in her arms, got into an earnest conversation with them. By the evening the maharaja had arrived from Patiala with Bryan, Attar Singh and Jivan Singh. All of them, closeted in the parlour, discussed the catastrophe that had taken them unawares and debated on the right step to be taken. In the course of the discussion, Betty had felt faint and was taken to bed. Minnie did not join the discussion. She remained in her daughter's room sitting forlornly beside the lifeless body now wrapped in a white sheet. The others continued their discussion which gained momentum with every passing minute. They talked until late at night and then dispersed. The guests were accommodated in the palace for the night. The following morning they would begin early.

The sky was still dark and Betty was still asleep when her mother came into the room softly and shook her awake.

'What's it, mother?' she mumbled sleepily. She was still under the influence of the sedative administered to her the evening before.

'We have to leave. Now.' There was an urgency in the vicereine's tone.

'Huh?' Betty stared uncomprehendingly. And then, hazily the events of the previous day came back to her mind. Her eyes grew wide with fear and she clutched her mother's arm.

'Don't leave me, mother,' she mumbled.

'No, I am taking you with me,' she said, deftly gathering her in her arms, wrapping her up in a hooded cloak.

Betty did not resist as her mother, with the help of the rajmata and Bibi Bachtiar, helped her downstairs and bundled her into the waiting coach. Only when the coach was to begin rolling down the drive did she mumble, 'And Kaka?'

'Hush,' her mother told her. 'He will be kept safely. You will soon see him.'

Bibi Bachtiar, from the coach window patted her hand, 'I will personally take care of his safety, don't worry.'

Betty sank back on the cushions and closed her eyes again. Her mother held her close as the viceroy's aide looked on grimly.

Amid swirling dark clouds the carriage rolled down the hill, carrying with it the British representative, the former viceroy's wife and daughter. The daughter the British crown had lost two and a half years ago was back in British custody once more.

From the window above, the maharaja looked down at the coach disappearing into the gloom. As he stared unblinking, a tear rolled down his bearded chin. The woman who had meant everything to him for almost three years was now going out of his life and he could do nothing about it. Motionless as a stone, he kept staring at the empty driveway long after the coach had disappeared down the winding road in the translucent grey mist.

As for Kaka, the little prince who was living the life of Kartar Singh, son of Attar Singh, he too was taken away from Jasbir and Harbir and handed over to Bibi Bachtiar, the maharaja's sister who bundled him up and took him away to Lahore to bring him up under her care. She insisted that Harbir and Jasbir would not be able to take care of the boy once they were married and had their own lives to live; as for Attar Singh, even if he should choose to remarry, his wife would probably not find it easy to bring up another woman's child; so, Kaka's aunt was convinced that he should grow up with his cousins. As a precautionary measure, the secret of his parentage would not be disclosed. He would have his upbringing and education in Lahore in a manner befitting royalty. Rajen would be able to visit him once in a while. At some point of time, when there was no physical danger to his life, he would once again take him back to Patiala to live in his rightful home, the Moti Bagh Palace. Until then, however, Bibi Bachtiar and Jivan Singh would take on the role of his parents. Kunwar Kartar Singh would be treated no different from their own sons.

The nearest church was in Simla and a coffin containing Gertie's body was taken there for burial. A sorrowing Charles Bryan consigned his daughter to the earth and returned to Chail, thence to Patiala with his grieving wife.

The royal palace of Chail had never before seemed so gloomy. There was tight-lipped secrecy in the air. No one spoke of what had happened in the palace. The news that was floated around and that reached Patiala was that Charles Bryan's daughter had passed away. But, that would mean the chhoti maharani, would it not? Gertie had not come to Patiala at all, so no one knew about her. And the chhoti maharani was missing. What exactly had happened? There was no one to give a convincing reliable answer, so rumours continued to float, multiply and get distorted. The silence surrounding the missing maharani crystallised and settled heavily over the palace like a thick shroud that no one had the courage to remove. It came to be accepted that Maharani Harnam Kaur had been summoned by the Almighty.

Wahe Guru!

THE LATER YEARS: 1896 TO 1900

Dreams have the tendency to fade into nothingness in the harsh light of the day. Chail Palace was a dream, an ephemeral idea turned into reality, a vision that was given a concrete shape especially for the chhoti maharani. Now that the chhoti maharani was no longer in their midst, there seemed no point in lingering on in the hills any longer. Rajen stayed on for a few weeks, hoping against hope that a horse-driven viceregal carriage would roll up the hill one day and bring back Betty. But when he finally got the message that Betty and her mother had boarded the ship for England, he resigned to his fate and sank into deep despair. Everything in the Chail Palace reminded him of her: the desk by the window where she sat scribbling into her diary, the mahogany dressing table where she brushed a hundred strokes into her hair religiously every night, the settee in the parlour where he had often surprised her when he returned early from the polo grounds, the two-seater swing under the cedar tree in the garden where they had spent many leisurely moments, and most of all the four-poster bed he had shared with her in the bedroom overlooking the Simla hills far beyond. Betty's unseen presence was everywhere in the palace. It was too much for Rajen to bear. For a while he seriously toyed with the idea of giving it away as a gift to his friend, Rana of Dholpur, who was also his maternal cousin. However, this transfer could not be effected without the sanction of the imperial power and when the British authorities heard of the plan, they strongly objected to the transaction. The Lieutenant Governor of Punjab, Sir Dennis Fitzpatrick, invoked Her Majesty's power and prevented the transfer from taking place: Chail property could not be handed over to another state. The maharaja realised the futility of his efforts but he could no longer continue living there and so decided to go back to the plains. In April of 1896, he closed the Chail Palace, left a caretaker in charge, and returned to Patiala with his men, grim and sorrowful.

Back in Moti Bagh Palace, he immersed himself in matters of the state, worked for his people night and day like a man possessed. He did not allow himself any time to think of the void in his life, of the pain in his heart, of the love that was lost. In his free time he consumed his energies on the polo ground or the cricket pitch. Anything, anything that would make him stop thinking of the sad gaping hole in his life.

For the next six months Maharaja Rajinder Singh dedicated every moment of his waking life to his people who saw and understood what was happening. They believed what they had been told: that Bryans' daughter had died just as the little Kaka had died earlier. In other words, they believed that their Maharani Harnam Kaur had died. Seeing the mask-like blank expression on their ruler's face, no questions were asked. They respectfully left him alone to cope with his loss, hoping that he would regain his balance in due time. The maharaja was young, virile and handsome; given time, he would bounce back and be his old self again, take another consort perhaps, and rekindle his interest in the physical pleasures of royal living. Youth has a resilience that does not allow it to be suppressed for too long.

As if in answer to the silent prayers of his people, life returned to the maharaja with a vengeance. The prolonged period of sorrow stretching across half a year was followed by a few boisterous years of unbounded promiscuity. As life limped back to normalcy in the royal palace, the maharaja too returned to his earlier flamboyant ways and the public breathed a sigh of relief, thinking that there would be happy times once more. Festivities in the palace reached a new high. On the slightest excuse there was a celebration: song and dance and music, gaiety accompanied by free flowing liquor. The Patiala peg made a comeback in a big way. There was never a lull on the polo grounds; the cricket pitch was constantly in use. The maharaja would quickly finish his daily routine and then attended to his favourite sports. Playing chess and bridge were new additions to his interests. His officers, in their zest to please their ruler, followed suit and engaged with him in all his interests, on the open sports field as well as in the private precincts of the card room.

He did not visit the badi maharani's chambers again, although to all appearances he maintained an appropriate formal relationship with her; the royal family moved to a new palace that he made in the midst of the Baradari Gardens. That was the Badi Baradari, close to the Chhoti Baradari which his late father had built, which became the royal home, in the midst of sprawling parks and grounds clustered with tall trees. The greenery of the new location had an ambience of its own and gradually, as the seasons turned, the deep wounds in the maharaja's heart began to heal. His thoughts turned again to the clinking of bangles, the gentle touch of feminine hands, and the soft jingle of anklets on bare marble floors. He did not have to seek too long or too hard for female company. His officers and servants were only too willing to understand his needs and bring him solace for his body and soul. The maharaja began to see a number of different young girls, each more charming and graceful than the other. The young ruler was following the whims of his heart and learning to savour the pleasures of life, beauty and sensuality once more. Although he did not enter into a formal matrimonial alliance again, he had what were called morganatic marriages and numerous physical intimacies, many of which resulted in offspring never formally acknowledged by the state although on a personal level the maharaja continued to be financially supportive of the women who had provided him solace. Physically, yes, he was involved with a number of women but his heart and his mind remained aloof. It was as though women were just a temporary balm for his tortured soul, to be used occasionally when the need arose. Most of the time he was his own master and remained engrossed in his work. His appearance did not give away the fact that under the poised demeanour was a tortured soul nursing a sad gaping hole in an aching heart.

This continued for a few months before the maharaja was again weary of this form of distraction which he began to consider frivolous. It did not work any more. He was bored of the women who came to him, of their eagerness to please, their ingratiating talk, their lack of intelligence, their tradition-bound outlook. Everything about them annoyed him. He realised it was time to turn his mind to something else. He returned to the polo ground, the cricket pitch, and the billiard table. Once again he immersed himself deep in these activities with an intensity that surprised his officers. They tried their best to keep pace with his mercurial interests but could not. He spent long hours at his office desk. His relationship with the British had improved ever since he had allowed Betty to return; the communication gap was bridged again. He would ride out for meetings with the British officials – sometimes to Simla because the ban on his entry into the summer capital had long since been lifted, and sometimes to a middle ground, either in Kasauli or in Kalka, to discuss issues of governance. More than once, the new viceroy, Lord Elgin, himself came to Patiala to meet the maharaja. His attitude was by and large supportive and the British officer sent positive reports to the English monarch of the maharaja's contribution to governance in India.

Particularly in the frontier wars with Afghanistan the maharaja's support to the British was highly appreciated. In 1897 the imperial troops were deployed in Mohmand and Tirah expeditions against the Pashtun and the Afridi tribes in the North-West Frontier Province. Rajinder Singh lent his support and served in person with the British commander, Major General Edmond Elles. The expedition was successful and the imperial government, to show its appreciation, awarded the maharaja the coveted Grand Cross of the Star of India, an honour which he accepted without getting too excited about it. Nothing excited him any more. He felt as though something vital in him had died and that he had become an unthinking, unfeeling machine that could work, work, and only work.

On auspicious days, along with the rajmata, he continued to visit the family gurudwara and dole out massive quantities of gold and silver in charity, along with clothes and food. He focused on establishing educational institutions. Mahindra College, which was set up by his father in 1875, was a special beneficiary of his benevolence, as were the schools and hospitals that he established. The laying of the first railway line connecting Patiala to Bhatinda and Rajpura was completed in his tenure. Presiding over the inauguration of the railway line, he whimsically brought back a bogey of the train as a souvenir. This bogey he proudly displayed on the open grounds opposite the Moti Bagh Palace.

In the annals of history it is recorded that those were difficult years because of several natural calamities: floods, famine, and plague. With his zeal and dedication he not only managed to surmount all hurdles but also transformed Patiala into a dynamic, progressive state.

Charles Bryan could see the young ruler burning himself out with excess work and tried to divert his attention to sport. He made an attempt to revive an old passion – hunting in the Bir, the nearby woods. One fine day, early on a Sunday morning, after the maharaja had returned from the gurudwara, Charles Bryan suggested that they should ride to the forest nearby where a river had overflowed its bank and flooded the neighbouring village. Hearing this, the maharaja set off with a few accompanying horsemen for a reconnaissance. Riding deep into the woods, they came to the gushing river, the flooded village, and the poor villagers sitting with their belongings on rooftops, trying to keep themselves dry. Immediate action was needed and the maharaja ordered his men to get to work, evacuate the villagers and plug the breach the best they could. A temporary solution now would be followed by a more permanent remedy the following day. Once the relief work began, the maharaja turned back with Charles.

Charles Bryan had had the foresight to bring some shotguns along. He had in mind the hope that he may be able to rekindle the young maharaja's interest in hunting. As they turned back from the village, he suggested a detour into the woods; perhaps they would spot a wild boar or a deer. The maharaja, surprised by the suggestion, agreed and they rode onward, looking for a prey. As they moved further into the thickly wooded Bir jungle, they heard a rustle in the leaves and espied a magnificent doe bounding away from them. Excited, they pursued the animal and aimed their guns for a kill but the doe was swift and managed to escape. The maharaja and Charles followed it for a while but seeing the setting sun turned back for the palace as they were unprepared for a longer stint in the Bir. Although the hunt had not been successful, the maharaja was reminded of his hunting escapades in the Annandale forest in Simla with the British officers and his appetite for hunting was revived. He told Bryan to have horses, men and dogs ready; they would soon go hunting.

But first something had to be done about the rising flood waters. The Patiala river was in an angry spate with the excessive monsoon. Its waters continued to rise well above the danger mark. Hutments in the low-lying areas close to the river were flooded. The population had moved to higher levels and were living in makeshift tents. Maharaja Rajinder Singh rode to the river bank personally and surveyed the floods. He heard stories of the people, their losses and sorrows, commiserated with them and promised to do something about it. But what? He returned to the palace and sat in serious discussion with his mother, debating on the action to be taken. That was when the rajmata told him of a similar incident that had taken place half a century ago: the story of a previous flood that had come down to her by word of mouth from her husband, the previous ruler, who in turn had got it from his grandfather, when he was a young boy. The half-remembered tale narrated the story of a long-drawn flood in the Patiala region and the visit of a faqir who had sat under the Dukhnivaran tree and advised the local people to tell the then maharaja that the angry waters of the river would subside only if he personally went to the river, prayed on the banks and gave an offering of gold to the raging waters. The story circulated in the city from mouth to mouth until it reached the ears of the maharaja who by then had despaired of finding a way to curb the flooding waters. Intrigued by the novel suggestion he decided to give it a try; so he rode up to the river bank on his horse, prayed with folded hands to the river that his people may be spared and then, taking off his gold ring, he threw it into the foaming waters. Thereafter, he returned to the palace.

'And did it work?' Rajinder Singh asked his mother, incredulous.

'It actually did,' she replied. 'The waters subsided, the river receded. I do not know how it happened, but it worked. You could try it. It might work again.'

Rajinder Singh did not give much credence to the story but he felt it was his duty to do something for his people in their hour of need; besides, he had nothing to lose, so he decided to follow the example of his ancestor. He sent for his horse and rode to the river bank. From atop a bridge fording the river he looked down at the swirling waters and muttered a prayer under his breath. Then he took off a gold chain that he wore around his neck and let it fall into the rushing waters. This done, he turned his horse around and rode back. He did not have much hope of the situation improving but, to his surprise, the next morning his men reported that the river had receded and was flowing in its normal course again; homes that had been evacuated in the flood were being occupied once more. The people had heard of their ruler's sacrifice of a little gold for the common good and were grateful. Their loyalty to their leader was further strengthened. As for the maharaja, he went to the gurudwara to pay obeisance and thanked the Gurus for standing by him at the critical juncture.

Cricket, along with horse-racing and polo, continued to be the maharaja's undiminished passion. He organised cricket matches in Patiala and also took the Patiala Eleven to distant places like Lucknow, Poona and Bombay, where tournaments were held, in which the Patiala team was invariably the winner. They brought back a number of trophies, all of which were proudly displayed in the Baradari residence. The maharaja's reputation as a sportsman spread far and wide. Simultaneously, he turned his attention to wrestling and brought the acclaimed wrestler Gama to the Patiala court, fixing a generous allowance for him. Gama successfully participated in wrestling matches across the country and came to be called 'Rustam-i-Hind' and 'Rustam-i-Zaman'. Other spheres of art, music, for instance, were also patronised. In earlier times, in the reign of Maharaja Narinder Singh, his grandfather, classical music was encouraged at the royal court and musicians and singers occupied an exalted place. Ustad Mian Tan-Ras-Khan from the Mughal court, who was also known as 'Qwal Bacha' was a frequent visitor at the Patiala Darbar along with his equally famous pupil, Bhai Kalu Rababi who belonged to the Anandpur Rababi family. His sons, Ali Baksh and Bade Ghulam Ali Khan, as well as Ustad Fateh Ali Khan, were brought to the royal court as was the singer Goki Bai. Under the maharaja's benevolent patronage the Patiala Gharana flourished, reaching the pinnacle of its glory.

In the year 1897, when the maharaja lent assistance to the British army in the Afghan war, he vindicated himself and returned to their good books, convincing the rulers of his goodwill; the ban on his entry to Simla was revoked and the Patiala cricket team was invited to play with the English Eleven at Annandale. In turn, he invited them to his palace in Patiala, an invitation that the viceroy graciously accepted. The viceroy, along with his team, visited the royal city of Patiala and was treated with so much of style and magnanimity that they all went back impressed and sent favourable reports to Her Majesty.

October 1900 marked the completion of a decade of Maharaja Rajinder Singh's full-fledged rule, not counting the fourteen years when he ruled under the Council of Regency. He was still young, just twenty-eight, but he had accomplished much in this brief span and it was evident that he was at the peak of his career. He was confident that he had again won the confidence of the ruling British as their strongest supporter on the Indian subcontinent. He had worked hard to win back their goodwill. Deep in his heart of hearts he nurtured a secret wish that one day Her Majesty would relent and he would be reunited with Betty, bring back Kaka, his little prince, from Lahore and live a happy, contented life with them. This dream kept him going through the long lonely years when ostensibly he remained immersed in state affairs but in his private moments, he desperately tried to fill the emptiness of his life with surrogate pleasures – wine, women, the playground and the race course.

Dussehra came and went. As usual, a massive celebration was organised at Qila Mubarak. The royal family attended in full force along with the officers and their families. The maharaja sat next to the rajmata, presiding over the function. He lit the arrow that was fired at the towering replica of Meghnath and watched it go up in flames. Then he set fire to the effigies of Kumbhakaran and Ravana. A resounding applause rose to the skies as the effigies smoldered and came down in a heap of ash. The roll of drums was followed by dancing groups in colourful traditional outfits doing the bhangra. Feasting and merry-making was the order of the day. It continued late into the night even after the maharaja and his mother returned to the palace.

In the same manner, Diwali was celebrated with zest and fervour. The Moti Bagh Palace, the gurudwara, the new Rajinder Kothi where the family now lived in the Baradari Gardens, the Qila Mubarak and the Sheesh Mahal were all brightly illuminated. The entire city was caught up in the spirit of the festival, decorated with flowers and garlands. Festivity and prayer marked the occasion. The royal household was in its most charitable avatar, giving alms and donations generously to the poor, the lame and the handicapped lined up outside the gurudwara. The staff, the officers and their families, too, got their share of gifts. Cheers for the maharaja reverberated through the royal city. There seemed to be peace, plenty and goodwill all around.

Appearances, however, can be deceptive. This was the outer calm, the organised, progressive exterior of the state with the maharaja in full control of the situation, making up his own rules and implementing them as he saw fit. As the benevolent dictator he had the appreciation of the majority of his people but it does not require more than a handful of discontented minority to brew trouble. Under the calm exterior was a seething, volatile current that could erupt at any moment – the way it had erupted earlier with the supposed deaths of Rajkumar Richard Ram Rahim and his mother, the chhoti maharani. This subterranean evil force was biding its time, plotting and planning, awaiting an appropriate moment to unleash its fury once more, this time with a cold and calculating finality. It did not have to wait long.

The Council of Regency was now a defunct power. Formerly it had occupied a special place in the politics of the royal house of Patiala. It comprised a small coterie of the topmost ministers of the state who were not only well-connected but also the most powerful and had the largest following in their area of governance. This council had taken charge when Rajinder Singh, at the age of four, was appointed the maharaja on the death of his father. For the next fourteen years, until the maharaja attained the age of eighteen and was given full powers by the British representative in India, the council had collectively governed the state. Once the reins of the kingdom were passed on to the maharaja, the council had become redundant. Rajinder Singh had tried to be fair to the members of the Council; he had given them small fiefdoms which they could rule more or less independently, and tried to involve them in all important decision-making. However, although they were part of all discussions, the action taken ultimately depended on the maharaja's sweet will. He would listen to them with all civility but finally have his own way. This had been going on from the day he took complete control in 1890 and it was becoming progressively more pronounced, thus adding to the collective chagrin of the ministers. They were the king-makers, they had protected the maharaja in his minority years, taken care of his education and upbringing, and run the state for fourteen years but now they were being marginalised. Their resentment was great indeed.

There were other disgruntled elements, too. Members of the badi maharani's maternal home, in particular her brothers, were unable to come to terms with the manner in which their sister was now marginalised in the royal household; they were unyielding in their hatred and they had vowed to take revenge. Although the chhoti maharani and her son were both out of the way now, their desire for vendetta remained unassuaged because the maharaja continued to be indifferent towards their sister. Together with the Council of Regency, they looked for an opportunity to get even with the maharaja. So great was their hatred that they would stop short at nothing. If the reasons for the council's acrimony were mainly political, those of the badi maharani's kin were purely personal. However, they were aware of the fact that the British rulers were very favourably disposed towards the maharaja, so they were afraid of incurring colonial wrath and could not come out openly in confrontation with the state of Patiala. For this reason they simply cooled their heels, biding their time for the right moment to strike. As a strategy, they had begun visiting Patiala with gifts for their sister, the maharaja and the rajmata. Win over the enemy before you strike him was their motto. Unsuspecting, the maharaja responded with civility, inviting them to partake in their family meals, festivals and even the weekly shikaars.

HUNTING IN THE BIR

Making a big comeback, shikaar was once more included in the maharaja's regular activities. Every Friday afternoon he would set out entourage for the nearby Bir, the thickly wooded forests. It was an elaborate affair – the horses, the dogs, the cooks, the grooms, the food and drinks, the entire paraphernalia went along with the maharaja for the hunt. The maharaja's favourite hunt was the wild boar; with his men he would chase it, surround it and then impale it with his spear. On this particular day, 8 November 1900, on the day following Guru Nanak Jayanti, the maharaja instructed Charles Bryan to prepare for boar hunting the following day. Bryan was generally in charge of the food and the horses and always accompanied the shikaar trips but on this occasion his wife, Minnie, was rather unwell and he wanted to stay by her side. Putting another trusted servant, Sardar Surahiwala, on duty, Charles Bryan asked the maharaja to excuse him. Rajinder Singh was not happy about it but he did not say anything because Sardar Surahiwala was equally trustworthy and would handle his duties efficiently, the way he always did.

Sardar Surahiwala was an institution in himself. He had been in the service of the royal household ever since he was a young boy of eight. The maharaja's late father, Maharaja Mahendra Singh, had taken a fancy to Karamjeet Singh – that was his real name – when he had first seen the lad performing the bhangra at a Basant Festival outside the Moti Bagh Gurudwara. Something about the wide-eyed, endearing innocence of the boy had touched his heart and he had taken him under his wing. That was three decades ago. Karamjeet began as a trainee in the royal kitchen, and then gradually rose to the rank of chief bearer and bartender. As a boy he was very fair and pink, with a slender graceful, almost feminine throat – like a long-necked vase or a *surahi*. The name Surahiwala was initially used in a jocular sense, the other menfolk of the kitchen making fun of the ruler's new favourite. With time, however, the boy had won the respect and admiration of the kitchen staff with his quiet efficiency and pleasant demeanour. He had continued working for the new ruler and now, at the age of thirty-eight, he was among the most trusted servants of the maharaja and personally supervised the food and drinks of the royal family. Always elegantly turned out, formally dressed in immaculately maintained clothes, he had also won the admiration of the badi maharani who would get him to tie the *pagri* of the young prince Bhupinder Singh, a task that he was pleased to carry out, no matter how busy he was with other assignments.

Sardar Surahiwala it was, who was entrusted to take care of the maharaja's food, wines and liquor on this ill-fated hunting trip, a duty that he gladly accepted, not realising what fate had in store for him.

The hunting expedition began with a lot of fanfare: the roll of drums, tom-toms and horns echoed through the city as the horses began to clatter out of the palace towards the Bir, the maharaja leading the troupe with his officers and senior ministers, and the kitchen department bringing up the rear. Sardar Surahiwala, however, was delayed at the last minute. He had come down suddenly with gripes in his stomach. Clutching on to his abdomen, he had rushed to relieve himself. However, the gripes would not go and he collapsed again. Seeing him double up in pain, his family had forced him back into the house and sent for the doctor. By the time the doctor arrived Surahiwala was throwing up violently and had fallen unconscious. It was probably something he ate, the doctor said, gave him a stiff dose of medicine, told the family to watch over him, and left. Surahiwala remained out of his senses, cold and sweating for the next few hours. When he came to his senses again, he was in a state of panic – he had been entrusted with a duty but he had let the maharaja down. How could he forgive himself? His family, however, held him back and sent a message to Charles Bryan, explaining the sudden crisis. Bryan, on getting the news, decided to leave his ailing wife's bedside and join the maharaja's hunting troupe. Saddling his horse immediately, he too set off for the Bir. It was then almost dark. Very soon the maharaja would take a break and ask for his food and drinks.

The Bir extended for many miles and the maharaja and his men had gone far deep into the woods in pursuit of their quarry. The wild boar they had sighted dodged them, ducked and ran through the thick foliage, and they rode long and hard in hot chase. Finally, just as the sun was about to set, they managed to round up the animal, a colossal wild female boar with huge teats. As they formed a circle around the animal, she emitted blood-curdling screams. Once she was cornered, the maharaja, with a loud war cry, threw his spear with full force at her. The spear struck her in the neck and the boar let out a long spine-chilling howl as blood spurted out. She darted about with greater desperation. There was no chance of escape as she was surrounded by horsemen who plunged their spears into her one by one until she, with louder and more terrified howls, sank to the ground, her legs twitching spasmodically as she gasped her last. A triumphant cry resounded through the Bir and the grooms stuck the gore-dripping boar on a pole and carried her away, a trophy now to be roasted and eaten by all. The maharaja, exultant, turned back to the camp with his men. They would now rest and enjoy a couple of Patiala pegs before dinner was served. A pity, he thought, that Charles Bryan was not with them. True, there were the other officers but something in their ingratiating manner always made him feel ill at ease.

When the horses were taken away to be fed and groomed, the maharaja, in his tent, asked for Surahiwala. He was told that the trusted servant had not shown up. That was rather strange, thought the maharaja as he allowed his grooms to help him wash and change into a fresh set of clothes. But he was tired after the long chase and soon bodily fatigue overpowered his mind; he thought no more of it. Sinking back against the pillows, he reached out for his glass, and asked a serving boy to press his aching calves. It had been a long day and he was pleasantly tired. Soon they would bring in the cooked wild boar and he would savour it with his whisky. Taking one long sip from his glass, he felt relaxed and closed his eyes. Soon his senior officers would join him and sit around, joking and laughing, trying to please him. He wished Bryan were with him.

Suddenly, in his semi-inebriated state, the maharaja realised how much Charles Bryan meant to him, how the man had stood up for him whenever the occasion demanded, and how he had bailed him out from time to time, whenever he was in trouble. Thinking of the generosity with which the Bryans had kept Betty in their house for several months, a smile came to the maharaja's lips. Betty. Where was Betty now? Would he ever meet her? Would he ever claim her as his own again? Betty and Kaka? How was he doing in Lahore? The apple of his eye whom he was forced to send away into hiding. He had last visited him just before Diwali with new clothes and gifts. His lovely blue-eyed boy. His and Betty's.

Suddenly, he opened his eyes. He was alone in the tent with an unfamiliar midget-sized boy massaging his legs. There was only one thought in his mind: I must get her back, no matter what. Betty would come back to the palace, so would Kaka. They would live together as one happy family. He would go and bring them back personally. He would ride out on Sultan, put Kaka on the saddle with him, and bring him back to his rightful place. And then he and Kaka and Betty would go for long drives in their motor car. In the monorail. He would teach Kaka how to ride. They would play cricket and polo together. They would play billiards. They would race horses. They would travel the world together. London and Paris and Vienna and Berlin and....

The maharaja's brain was beginning to fuzz again. With half-shut eyes he held out his empty glass; someone filled it up again and he raised it to his lips, taking in the burning liquid in long, greedy gulps.

The tent swam around him. He leaned back and looked up. In the colourful pattern on the ceiling he could see a pair of blue eyes floating in a frame of golden ringlets, looking down at him. And then another pair of blue eyes in a baby-face with a toothless smile. Betty and Kaka were smiling at him. The maharaja smiled back at them and mumbled: 'I'm coming for you. You know that? Tomorrow.' Why wait? Tomorrow he would dash off a missive to the viceroy, telling him he wanted Betty back. He would not take it lying down any more. He would name his terms. Patiala had been loyal to the British for much too long. Was it not time for them to pay back now? Reward him for his loyalty? Give him back his lovely Betty.

He took another long draught from his glass and shut his eyes. The smile lingered on his face. He was dreaming of the garden swing in front of a palace on a high mountain top. It was a grey, misty morning with clouds wafting through the garden. He and Betty were sitting on the swing; she had Kaka in her lap and was gently curling a golden strand of hair around her finger as she hummed softly under her breath. As the baby drifted into sleep, she looked up at the maharaja through those wide blue eyes and smiled. He smiled back at her and closed his eyes, trying to capture forever that fleeting moment before it faded into nothingness.

Maharaja Rajinder Singh smiled and lay back to rest on his pile of cushions, dreaming of a happy reunion with his loved ones.

This is how Charles Bryan found him when he finally reached the camping ground. The maharaja was not asleep but dead. An empty glass lay overturned by his side but there was no bottle to be seen, no servants, no grooms, absolutely nobody around the maharaja's tent who knew what had happened, who could explain the situation. Distraught, he ran around the camp, looking for help and found every single person busy doing something else, apparently ignorant of what had happened. Each individual he spoke to had a convincing alibi. As Bryan looked around for a reason, for some clues, for someone he could talk to, the royal body turned stiff and blue. There was no longer any doubt: it was not alcohol but a strong lethal drink that had been administered to him. The maharaja's story was finally over.

While Charles and Minnie Bryan grieved in private and Sardar Surahiwala beat his chest in grief, the Council of Regency exulted as it once again came back to power and took control of the situation. They appointed the young prince Bhupinder Singh, who was then barely nine years old, as the *de jure* maharaja. His mother, the badi maharani, emerged from the margins as the new rajmata while the old matriarch receded to the background. The council resumed its unchallenged control of the state for the next ten years until the prince attained the age of maturity and was invested with full powers by the British Regent.

Maharaja Rajinder Singh's rule passed into the annals of history.

KARTAR

REVELATIONS

Attar Singh sighed and was silent for a long time. I could see that it had not been easy for him to recall a painful personal tragedy enacted in a difficult period in the history of the state.

'Although you were being brought up in Lahore, I have always thought of myself as your father,' said Attar Singh softly. There was a look of sadness on his face as he was transported back to the time when he had suddenly lost his first child.

But soon he controlled himself and smiled again: 'I lost my first child but gained another. You. I have always thought of you as my son. You, Kunwar Kartar Singh, are my legal heir and we will let it remain so.'

I did not know how to react to the generosity of this large-hearted man so I remained silent. The grandfather clock in the hall ticked on noisily. The last embers of the *angeethi* were burning low. We sat in silence for a while. Then I spoke again.

'Then how did you allow me to be sent to Lahore?' I asked.

'To Lahore? Well, you had to go there sooner or later, to study at Aitchison's because that is where all the young men of the royal family go. In this case, however, you were taken away from me much earlier because of a sudden turn of events. It could not be otherwise. Your personal safety was involved.'

Attar Singh told me that he was one of the four guardians appointed to take care of me. The first was, of course the maharaja himself, who would supervise my upbringing but from a distance. The second was my baba, Jivan Singh of Lahore. Attar Singh was the third.

'And the fourth?' I asked.

'Maharaja Jagatjit Singh of Kapurthala,' replied Attar Singh. 'He is very attached to our maharaja.'

I noted that he still spoke as though Maharaja Rajinder Singh were still around.

'Now that you have come of age and know what the truth is, I suggest you should pay him a visit too. He may have some more information that may be of interest to you.'

He rose from the couch, turned down the lamp and walked slowly out of the room, as though drained of all energy. I followed suit, heading for the room they had given me for the night. To my surprise, I found it unoccupied. Perhaps Attar's wife, thinking of my convenience, had taken the boys into her room for the night.

I lay in bed staring at the ceiling for a long time before I fell into a fitful sleep, still musing over the extraordinary story

I had heard. I mused over the various stages of my life: first, a baby in the maharaja's palace, born to the chhoti maharani; second the supposed son of Attar Singh of Amritsar; third, the adopted child of Jivan Singh of Lahore; and fourth, the ward of the Maharaja of Kapurthala. I realised that I was perhaps one of the extremely rare individuals in the world who had four different sets of parents at different stages of his life. Not that I had any choice in the matter. I had changed hands almost as though I were an unwanted burden that should be got rid of before it weighed them down. As though I were a ball of fire that would scorch my parents or guardians if they held me for too long. It was like a game of passing the parcel, one set of guardians handing me over to the next. Washing their hands off me. Putting me out of their lives. And out of their minds too. Such had been my fate. Whatever did I do to deserve it? I wish I knew.

I gathered most of the details of my story from Attar Singh on that fateful night. The rest I managed to piece together over the years, a clue, a hint, a scrap of information at a time from various sources. Then I put together all the fragments I had gathered and tried to arrive at a complete picture. The picture has many gaps and holes but I can now see something of a pattern in it.

According to Attar Singh's story, I was a little prince who had been sent away following an intrigue in the palace. Although my parents, the maharaja and his wife, loved me very much, for political reasons, they were unable to keep me with them. I was not safe – my life was in danger. I was a prince – the thought kept going round my brain. I was a prince, it was unsafe to keep me in the palace – so they tossed me out to the seas – the proverbial baby thrown out with the bathtub.

Bibi was actually my bui. Mamu was my father. Rajen mamu? The tall burly uncle of my childhood who came like Santa Claus and brought me sweets and gifts. Rajen mamu piling us up in his car and driving around the city. Rajen mamu on horseback, handsome and flamboyant like a meteor, dying an untimely unnatural death. Rajen mamu, my father?

'Are you serious?' I had asked.

'Yes,' he had said in an infinitely gentle tone.

Vaguely, from the musty recesses of the past came a dimly recollected memory of bibi weeping over me as I lay in bed half-asleep; bibi telling me that Rajen mamu had died. Bibi calling me a poor unfortunate baby. Bibi mumbling that I was orphaned. So, was this the truth? Then how did Attar Singh come into the picture? I could see the pattern and yet not see it. It perplexed me no end. How could it be? How could I, just an ordinary boy turning eighteen in the city of Lahore, be such an important peg in such an extraordinary story?

Maharajas, Attar Singh told me, are a special breed. They can marry more than once. They can install their wives in their palaces or forts as their maharanis if they so wish. BUT – and this was a big but – if they marry below their status then their wives are denied queenly rights and so are their children. Wives and children of such unions have no claim on royalty, no right of inheritance, and no titles coming their way. Such marriages – below the royal status – are 'morganatic' marriages. Morganatic marriages or mockery marriages? Was it some kind of a joke? I confess I was unfamiliar with the term before Attar Singh introduced me to it.

At that point of time the tale was too fantastic for me to absorb. It just would not sink in. It would take me awhile to realise that the story I had heard was in fact my own story. It would take me a longer while indeed to get used to thinking of myself as RRR or as the rajkumar, or as anything other than Kartar as I was known in Lahore. Attar Singh of Amritsar was undeniably the most important witness to the truth I was seeking. The rest of the story, along with some very unexpected details, came to me piecemeal from diverse sources. A major source of information was the diary that he gave me along with the bundle of loose papers tied up with a string. In those papers, among the many official and semi-official documents that I saw, one of them stood out. It had five distinct signatures: the maharaja's, the rajmata's, the viceroy's and two others that I did not recognise. Probably Attar Singh's and Maharaja Jagatjit Singh's. This was the deed which they had together signed at Chail, shortly before sending chhoti maharani back with her mother. In this deed, clearly stated were the clauses that were to shape my later life. As I read through the itemised list I could feel the rush of blood in my head. My heart started pounding and I found myself covered with hot sweat. Five people, sitting at a table had bartered away my life, just like that. How could they do it?

Clause 1 stated that the chhoti maharani of Patiala would be returned by the Maharaja of Patiala to Her Majesty the Queen of England. 'Returned' – as though she were a piece of furniture that had been borrowed by the state of Patiala. 'Returned' – as though she had been forcibly taken to Patiala against her will.

Clause 2 stated that the Rajkumar Richard Ram Rahim, henceforth referred to as RRR, would not be told the secret of his parentage. RRR, who is now known as Kunwar Kartar Singh, son of Attar Singh of Amritsar, would be formally adopted by Jivan Singh and Bachtiar Kaur of Amritsar and he would be brought up as their child.

Clause 3 was a bit unexpected. It made it mandatory for RRR, alias Kunwar Kartar Singh, to grow up as a devout *keshdhari* sardar. He would not cut his hair or beard and he would wear a turban all his life.

Clause 4 forbade RRR alias Kunwar Kartar Singh to leave the Indian subcontinent. He was never ever to try going to England; he was never to seek his biological mother, the chhoti maharani Harnam Kaur, alias Beatrix.

Clause 5 stated that RRR's upbringing and education would be looked after jointly by the Maharaja Jivan Singh, Attar Singh and Jagatjit Singh. They would ensure that he received education fit for a prince.

Clause 6 dealt with financial arrangements for RRR's upkeep. It made it mandatory for the State of Patiala to allocate a certain sum for RRR's education and future prospects. This privy purse was to be given to RRR even if he was being brought up in a city other than Patiala. Until he attained the age of eighteen the responsibility of claiming the money would be the guardian's but thereafter RRR alias Kartar Singh would deal directly with the State of Patiala.

There were some more clauses, too, pertaining to continued cordial relations between the British rulers and the royal house of Patiala. My attention, however, remained fixed on the first six listed in the document. I could feel a surge of anger rise inside me. I was angry with the British government, angry with the world, angry with circumstances that I had no control over, angry because the very people who were mine, who were supposed to own me and look after me, had let me down – either by giving me away as though in charity, or by dying, or by some other quirk of fate – leaving me at the mercy of a callous, uncaring, wide world.

This is how I was orphaned in more ways than one while still a baby. Abandoned. Left alone to fend for myself even before I was old enough to do anything about it. I was kept in the dark all these years. I thought I was living a normal life, growing up the way other boys my age were growing up. But this revelation made me realise that all along I had been groping, stumbling, feeling my way through endless labyrinths. I had never felt so alone and rudderless in the world. No ship, no oar, no support. Only a host of questions that kept going round in my mind like a whirlwind that never died. Why? Why? Why? There was still a veil of ignorance hanging over my eyes, preventing me from seeing the whole picture. So I would have to grope for some more evidence – stray hints and clues, a little pointer here, a sign there, which would enable me to piece together the whole picture, which would narrate to me the entire story of my life and also the reasons why the story developed the way it did.

All through the night I remained in the grip of conflicting emotions. In my saner moments, when I was more composed, more in control of myself I realised the inevitability of whatever happened, of the incidents that had taken me from one stage of my life to another, each stage being left behind like a chapter closed forever. The inevitability would strike me time and again. How else could it be otherwise, the situation being what it was? I, Kartar Singh, in my newly discovered identity as Sri Richard Ram Rahim Singh, realised that no one was to blame in the entire story. It simply was writ and had to be. In this story RRR had died but Kartar was condemned to live on and wonder why.

The diary filled up some gaps in the story. Basically, it narrated the same tale but from a woman's perspective. It also explained the large brooch studded with the ruby. It was the maharaja's first gift to Betty and she had worn it often pinned on her dresses. The blue silk was a scarf that she owned, so Attar Singh had told me. The sheaf of papers and the documents had been passed on to him by the maharaja at a later date for safe-keeping. Now that I had been initiated into the story, these items belonged to me.

What now? I wondered.

'You need to go to Kapurthala, my son,' Attar Singh told me the next morning. 'Stay with us as long as you wish but the maharaja wanted you to meet with his friend Jagatjit.'

That reminded me of bibi's directive to me – to go and meet Attar Singh in Amritsar – and I wondered what more surprises life would have for me.

KAPURTHALA

From Amritsar I did not go back to Lahore immediately. Instead, I headed for Kapurthala with a note for Maharaja Jagatjit Singh from Attar Singh. I went alone and thought I would return alone to Lahore after the meeting. Little did I know that I would not be alone on my return from Kapurthala. With me would be my bride, the niece of the maharaja. This was ordained, although I had no inkling of it when I headed in that direction. My halt in Kapurthala was longer than I expected. I could afford to extend my stay as the college in Lahore was closed for the winter vacation and would reopen only after Lohri.

I had never been to Kapurthala before. I had simply heard about its splendour from bibi and baba. In their conversations they often mentioned Maharaja Jagatjit Singh whom I treated as yet another character from a fairy tale because all his exploits seemed to be extraordinary. Never had I thought I would actually go to his city to meet him in person. Growing up in Lahore, Kapurthala was distant enough to be unreal, so was Maharaja Jagatjit. Invariably his name and that of Maharaja Rajinder Singh, whom I still thought of as Rajen mamu, were mentioned in the same breath. The only difference was that one was still alive, the other dead. I had heard stories of their colourful personalities, their flamboyance, their riotous youthful days in the Simla hills, the summer frolics at the Viceregal Lodge, and the sojourns in the Chail Palace. Now, armed with fresh knowledge of how close the two maharajas were, and how the ruler of Kapurthala had stood by Rajen mamu through thick and thin, I realised that Jagatjit was another important link in the story that was being unravelled before me, bit by bit. Meeting him was not only essential but also inevitable.

'A couple of rogues' and 'a pair of rascals' is how my Baba Jivan Singh would affectionately refer to the two erstwhile royal friends. On being asked to explain, he once regaled me with a number of stories of how much the two maharajas had in common, and how their fun-loving temperaments led them into similar scrapes from time to time. Not only were they the same age, their public lives had also followed a similar graph. Like Rajinder Singh, Jagatjit too had been placed on the throne while still a child: he was just five years old when his father, His Highness the Raja Kharak Singh had died. Like Rajinder Singh, he too had assumed full powers in the year 1890, on attaining the age of eighteen. Both had a passion for travelling and enjoyed taking time off to visit Europe whenever the opportunity arose. They were groomed in Western etiquette, had a fondness for opulence, for wine and women – particularly white-skinned women – and loved hunting, cricket, billiards and polo. Both had cordial relations with the British Empire and its regents and were recognised as supportive rulers of vassal states. To cap it all, the two were always in close communication with each other and would often ride up to the British summer capital together to join the imperial officers in their summer frolics. Invariably, when spending time together they would end the day stretched out before a fireside with whisky bottles scattered around them and grooms fussing over them.

My baba also referred to them as 'rascals' and 'daredevils', telling me how each would egg the other on to attempt crazy feats, particularly when they sojourned in Simla. For instance, if they saw a pretty young girl at the ball, there would be a wager: they would place a bet on which of them would be able to dance with her first. One would defy the other to take the first step towards the object of their attention. They would vie with each other, coming up with witty pick-up lines to win the attention of the English womenfolk. That was not always easy: on one occasion, during a glitzy dinner ball at the Viceregal Lodge, Rajinder Singh had dared his friend to dance with a particular cantankerous English lady well-known for her animosity towards brown skin. This woman was well past middle-age and had a perpetual scowl on the face, particularly when dealing with Indians who, according to her, needed to be put in their place all the time. Jagatjit Singh had scoffed at the idea of sweet-talking her at first but, when his friend egged him on, he took up the challenge with a mild protest: 'And what if she should bite me? Will you bite her back.' To which Rajinder Singh had jocularly placed his hand on his heart and assured him he would, slapped him on the back encouragingly, and sent him across the floor to the scowling woman. Accepting the challenge, and mustering up all his wits, Jagatjit had then approached the scowling lady and – as his friend watched in glee from the other end of the hall – actually managed to engage her in an interested conversation for a good half hour, much to everybody's surprise because her antipathy towards Indians was no secret. The scowl on the lady's face gradually faded as he talked to her in fluent French and English; it was then replaced by a smile, grudging and reluctant at first but soon turning almost genuine. Finally, to everyone's surprise, she had got up from her chair and allowed Jagatjit to lead her on to the dance floor. That was not all: it was believed that she, along with her attractive and very eligible daughter, subsequently paid him a visit in Kapurthala and enjoyed his generous hospitality for a week.

'Those two rascals could charm the birds off the trees,' I remembered my baba's words as I headed towards Kapurthala.

I had planned to be in Kapurthala for just a couple of days. I thought I would talk to Jagatjit Singh the way I had talked to Attar Singh and then return to Lahore to resume my studies. That was the winter break in Aitchison's and I had imagined I would return to Lahore well in time before the college reopened. Once back, I would again be immersed in studies. The length of my stay was thus intended to be a short one. However, that was not meant to be. I stayed there for three whole weeks and this extended stay was purely by accident. Had I not flown into a mad rage the very next morning after reaching the palace, perhaps I would have returned to Lahore within a couple of days. Moreover, I would have returned single, a bachelor, and a *brahmachari*. But again, that was not to be. It was so ordained that I would go on a rampage in an alien home. I was destined to get so incensed that the very palace walls would quake with the violence of my tantrums and Jagatjit, out of his loyalty towards the former Maharaja of Patiala, Rajen mamu who was also my father, would take me in hand, din some sense into my head, keep me by his side until passions had cooled and I had become normal again. Finally, by the end of it, when the fit of mad rage subsided, it was again a part of a higher design that the bond between us would be so thick that he would even offer me a bride from his own family. Like so many other events in my life, this too was writ in my destiny, whether I liked it or not. So it was.

Kapurthala was a surprise. Although my mind, befuddled as it was with all the information I had gained in Amritsar, was in no condition to observe and comment on the architecture of the city, I did note that it seemed unusual, even European. Perhaps, it was the impact of the maharaja's European travels. Indeed, as they informed me at the palace, the maharaja was a Francophile who had modelled his palace after Versailles. It even bore a French name – the Elysee. A progressive and secular ruler, he wanted the best for his people, had set up philanthropic institutions, gardens, temples and mosques in the city, winning over the hearts of his subjects despite his eccentric whims and fancies.

The maharaja received me personally when I arrived at the palace, read the note given by Attar Singh and held me tight in a close embrace. Although he did not say much, his eyes told me that he was a man I could trust. He would know what was best for me and give me the right direction. But it was evident that he was in no hurry to talk; I could sense that he had something important on his mind. Ordering his servants to escort me to my chambers, he observed that I must be tired and should relax for a while; we would meet at dinner later in the evening. Not used to travelling, I was indeed tired. Moreover, the events of the last few days had exhausted me and I felt emotionally drained. I soon fell asleep in my room and woke up only when I heard a servant knocking on my door, telling me that the maharaja awaited my presence in the dining hall.

Next to the maharaja sat a young woman of extraordinary beauty, heavily bedecked in gold and diamond jewellery She was introduced to me as Prem Kaur, his fifth wife. I had never seen so beautiful a woman before. So graceful and yet so artless. Her movements were slow and almost rhythmic as she reached out for the food on her plate and conveyed it to her mouth in a slow, almost stylised dance motion. She spoke to the maharaja in an unfamiliar foreign language that sounded like French and seemed to be a strange blend of the west and the east. As the conversation proceeded I gathered that her original name was Anita Delgado, that she was of Spanish origin and was a small-time professional dancer before the maharaja took a fancy to her, brought her to the palace as his wife and gave her a more acceptable Indian name. It was evident that her middle-aged husband doted on her and that she enjoyed the attention. Her attitude towards me was one of casual curiosity. She was polite but I did not seem to merit much of her attention which was directed most of the time towards the maharaja and occasionally to a young boy seated opposite her. Later I was to discover that he was Karamjeet, the maharaja's son by his fourth wife, who had struck a happy rapport with his new stepmother.

Alcohol was being served along with the sumptuous dinner. When I said I did not drink, the maharaja guffawed.

'What! Aren't you your father's son? Come on, man, here's one for you. Let me initiate you into the grown-up world.' He poured out a drink and handed me a glass which I could not but accept.

I toyed with the glass, twirling it in my hands, not knowing what else to do.

'Be a man and drink it up, son,' he chided me again.

I brought the glass to my lips and pretended to drink. He saw through the game and laughed. I was sheepish and took a sip from the glass. And then another. And another.

The liquid burned all the way down to my belly. My brain sent me a warning message telling me I should stop as I was unaccustomed to drink. Seeing that the maharaja was distracted by his Spanish wife again, I put my glass away and concentrated on the food, the glittering apparel of my royal host and his paramour, the multicoloured chandeliers on the ceiling, and the hordes of servants hustling about the hall, serving food and drink. After this splendid repast, I wondered if the maharaja would be in the right frame of mind for a serious conversation.

Surprisingly, he was. He was as sober as daylight once the dinner was over and the lady hanging on his arm had kissed him on the cheek and departed, telling him not to be too late.

'Tell me, my son, what can I do for you?' he finally turned to me, reclining on a divan in the adjoining parlour, resting his elbow on a heavy bolster.

I sat on the edge of a huge carved chair facing him, unsure of what to say. That did not bother him as he seemed to be quite happy carrying on a monologue.

'Attar says you now know the truth of your parentage,' he continued. It was a statement, not a question.

'Yes, Your Majesty.'

A long pause. And then: 'Yes, it was a bit complicated, but could not be helped.'

And then: 'Rest assured, I will always be by your side if you need me. Rajinder Singh was very dear to me. You are equally dear.'

His eyes were moist. I wondered if it was the effect of the drink. Or was it genuine emotion?

Finally he said: 'You will carry on life like before. No change. It cannot be otherwise.'

I asked: 'Can I go to Patiala?'

'Why not? As Attar Singh's son, anytime. And as Jivan Singh's adopted child.'

'Can I see my mother?' I asked hesitantly. 'My biological mother.'

He shook his head. 'No, I am afraid not. She went back to England. Her Majesty's officers made us sign an agreement that you would not try to seek her.'

I was crushed. 'Does she even know I am still alive?' I asked.

'I don't know,' was the reply.

And then: 'In any case, it is better to let sleeping dogs lie. Why do you wish to unravel a past which has no relevance now? It would only cause problems.'

'Problems? Like how?'

'Hm-m-m. Well, for one, the British rulers would not allow it. Two, the lady in question probably has her own life now in England. She must be long married, perhaps the mother of six or seven children. Would you like to complicate matters for her? After all, like you, she too has been a pawn in a bigger game. Life has not been fair to her either.'

This was a new way of looking at the picture. So far I had merely been thinking of myself and how fate had betrayed me. I kept silent.

He continued: 'Have you heard of *Enoch Arden*?'

I had not.

'Tennyson. A poem by Alfred, Lord Tennyson. Enoch Arden leaves his wife and three children, goes looking for work. He is lost and missing for ten years, considered to be dead. When he finally returns he finds that his wife, thinking he was dead, is now happily married to his childhood friend, raising his children and also another one by her second husband. Seeing her happily settled in another home, Enoch feels it would be incorrect to disrupt her life again and so does not reveal his identity.'

I allowed the story to sink in.

'He dies of a broken heart,' continued Jagatjit, taking another sip from his glass.

A long pause and then he continued: 'It would serve no purpose, believe me. Today, you are well-respected in society – as Attar Singh's son and Jivan Singh's ward. If the truth came out, not only would you endanger your life again, you would also be treated as an outcast, a half-breed.'

I winced at that.

'Half English, half Sikh. That would make you a half-breed, would it not?'

I had no reply.

'Besides,' he told me, 'you need to remember that in our society no individual is an island. We are, each of us is, a part of a larger family, a part of society. You need to be accepted. You need to be one of them, not different from them.'

He paused for a while then continued: 'Today you are single. You can think only of yourself. But tomorrow you will have a family of your own. You will have daughters and would need to find grooms for them. What would you say then about your lineage? Would you say that your mother … .'

He did not complete the sentence but I was beginning to understand what he was trying to get at. Too confused to respond, I just sat there, listening to him in silence. His tone was gentle but he spelt out a few brutal facts that I had not been aware of fully. He made me realise all over again the inevitability of events that had taken place and the futility of trying to change the situation now. It would only mean more trouble. Better by far to reconcile to the circumstances and move on.

'Sleep over it, my lad, and you will understand that this is your only option, the only way to handle the situation. You are tired now, so am I. We will resume our conversation tomorrow,' he yawned wearily.

I got up to go. As I turned he called out again, 'Here, take this – you will need it.'

He held out the bottle of whisky that he had opened a while ago. It was still three-quarters full. I hesitated but he pushed it into my hand. At the doorway I lingered.

'What is it? Any questions?'

'Well,' I began, 'there is one point I cannot fully understand.'

'Well?' I had fallen silent so he prodded me on.

'Er-r. I know we are Sikhs and as Sikhs we abide by our faith and our customs. We take it for granted. But why did they have to spell it out in the agreement that I should grow up as a Sikh? That I should wear a turban and never cut my hair or beard? Why were they so concerned about me going against my own religion? I don't quite understand.'

Jagatjit halted at the doorway and looked me straight in the face. His eyes were serious.

'Son,' he said, 'have you seen pictures of yourself as a baby?'

As a matter of fact I had not.

'Have you any idea what you looked like without your beard and moustache?' he touched the thick growth on my face.

'No. Not really,' I did not know what he was getting at.

He continued: 'Your eyes are blue. As an infant you had your mother's clear pink skin. To all appearances you were not Indian. It would not be in their interest for you to be recognised as a souvenir of the British Regency. The turban, the facial hair would serve as a camouflage.'

Patting my shoulder he walked away, his words ringing in my ears.

I did not sleep that night. I could not. I was tortured. I tossed and turned. I asked myself a million questions but came up against a blank wall every time.

The room in which they had put me up was on the first floor. It had huge windows overlooking the palace grounds. As daylight streamed in I realised that I had been lying awake, staring at the ceiling all night long. I was hungry and looked around the room for something to eat. A bowl of fruit stood on the table. Apples, pears and a papaya. Next to it was a plate and a fruit knife. The palace was still quiet and it would be a while before any activity would begin in the kitchen. I reached out for the papaya and cut out slices to eat. The knife was sharp and my thoughts were elsewhere as I cut the fruit. A sharp pain brought me back to reality. I had cut the thumb of my left hand and drops of blood were dripping on to the floor. Bright red drops -- like rubies. Like the jewel wrapped up in the silk cloth left behind by an English woman for the man she loved, for the son she had abandoned.

Taking a piece of the drawstring from my cotton trousers I tied up my thumb the best I could and began eating the fruit.

Facing me was a huge mirror held up by an ornate wooden frame. I saw my face reflected in it. The face of a 'Souvenir of the British Regency' – is that what I had been told?

The eyes were bloodshot with lack of sleep, the hair which was normally hidden under a turban, was dishevelled. The beard, usually rolled and tied neatly under the chin, was loose and long. What was it that I had been told about my appearance? That it was more English than Indian. I peered closely into the mirror. The eyes were blue, no doubt. They had always been blue but I had not given it much thought before. The complexion – I had never thought of it but as I stared closely, it was more white than brown. I tried to imagine what it was like under the beard and the moustache.

The bottle of whisky that my host had given me stood on the table before me. I thought it would be nice to take a swig and drown the confusion in my brain.

As I took a big gulp I felt strangely comforted. Another gulp made me feel even better. Strange, I who had been a teetotaler all along was now drinking at this early hour in the morning, a time for morning prayers, a time for close proximity with the higher powers. With the Gurus. With God.

God? Was there a God? I felt helpless frustration rise within me again. Taking out the sheaf of papers that Attar Singh had given me, once again I read the clauses that were to determine my life. 'RRR, alias Kunwar Kartar Singh, to grow up as a devout *keshdhari* sardar. He will not cut his hair or beard and he will wear a turban all his life.' And the next clause; 'RRR alias Kunwar Kartar Singh will never leave the Indian subcontinent. He will never ever try going to England; he will never try and seek his biological mother....'

I felt blood pounding in my temples and took another swig from the bottle in my hand. Picking up the fruit knife I examined it carefully. It was sharp, no doubt, as my sliced thumb had discovered a little while ago. But was it sharp enough ...? I turned it over and wondered? Looking into the mirror again, I studied the face of the 'souvenir' left behind. What would it look like without the hair? Without the beard?

Reaching out for another swig from the bottle, I was surprised to find it empty. Had I really emptied it?

The knife in my right hand, I sat staring at my reflection in the mirror. Then, coldly, deliberately, my cut thumb still throbbing, I held my hair up with the left hand and brought the knife close to the roots. No, a little higher than the roots.

Using the knife like a razor, I slashed away at my hair. At first I went about it cautiously. But when the first of the tresses fell to the floor, I could feel a surge of anger within me again. Recklessly I hacked away at the hair on my head.

Who had the right to tell me how to live? Why should I allow an alien power to dictate the terms and conditions of my personal life?

By the time the sun was high up in the sky I was standing in a sea of long strands of hair, the remnants of which stood upright on my head, shorn and unkempt. Then I turned to the beard. I slashed and scraped long and hard until it was all gone except for an uneven stubble on the chin. And the moustache, too, was almost gone as I did the best I could to get rid of an appearance I had nurtured carefully all my life.

My task over, I scrutinised the reflection in the mirror again. The 'souvenir' was now transformed. The blue eyes – although bloodshot – stood out in the face. The skin under the stubble glowed fair and pink. There were minor cuts and bruises inflicted by the knife but the face was completely changed.

I felt the blood surge into my head with a blinding force. Picking up the empty bottle I smashed the mirror with a loud cry. The image of the 'souvenir' cracked into a million pieces but I did not stop at that. I kept smashing the mirror and as I struck it I called it names. I roared and screamed as loud as I could. The bottle was now in smithereens. I picked up a stool lying in the corner and threw it against the window with all my force, hurling abuses to the sky. And then I brought down the lamps and chandeliers, the paintings on the walls, the marble statues decorating the mantelpiece. All the time there was a deafening roar in my head and blood in my eyes. When I had thrown the last object I could lay my hands on, I threw myself against the wall, over and over again, banging my head against the wooden panels until I felt something warm and liquid running down my face. Then I think I must have passed out.

HARBANS KAUR

When I came to my senses I was laid up in bed in another room of the palace. There were a number of people walking around me on tiptoe, talking in hushed whispers. As I stirred, a ripple went through the room and they all gathered at my bed. It took me a while to recall where I was. As memory flooded back to me, I remembered my rampage in the guest room of the Kapurthala Palace and I was ashamed. I tried to sit up but a pair of sturdy arms held me back and an attendant told me to take it easy. My head hurt; I touched it and felt a bandage on my forehead.

How long had I been this way? Nobody answered my question. Instead they brought me some food and drink and told me I needed nourishment. There were four of them who treated me with great deference and they all seemed to be servants of the royal palace. They told me that the maharaja had been looking in daily and would come again to see me in the evening. This meant that I had been laid up that way for several days. The thought made me uncomfortable, as though I were guilty of a breach of a code of conduct. As a guest, after all, I had to maintain a certain decorum which I had failed to observe. In my fit of uncontrolled anger I had broken the laws of hospitality.

I told them I needed to relieve myself and an attendant, a young boy, rushed to my side to help me to the toilet. As I got off the bed I found I was doddering. My knees buckled under me and the boy gave me support. Slowly, with his help, I walked across to the washroom. There, after I had finished emptying my bladder, he helped me wash my hands at a basin in the corner. As he poured water from a jug, I looked up and caught an unfamiliar reflection in the glass. That could not be me. I saw a head with a bandage across the forehead. On the crown, there was neatly cut soft brown hair; the beard and moustache covering the face were gone; the skin on the cheeks was smooth and pink; the eyes shone blue in a wan face. I realised that it was my reflection in the mirror, me minus my turban, minus my beard and moustache.

The attendant saw the question mark on my face and explained: 'The maharaja sent for the barber who gave you a haircut and shave. You have been injured and out of your senses for four days. We have been looking after you.'

Sponged and changed, I allowed myself to be led back to bed and waited for the evening when the maharaja would visit me.

To cut a long story short, my host, the maharaja came to see me that evening and every single evening during the ten days I spent in bed recuperating. He was kind, to put it very mildly. He could sense that I was feeling sheepish at the way I had behaved and magnanimously forgave me for it. Despite the many demands on his time he would spend an hour talking to me in a kind, fatherly manner, showing he cared, making me feel that I should not feel alone or rejected or abandoned. He did not talk about my shorn hair. It did not seem to matter at all to him. He was more concerned that I should get back to normal life once more. When I was better, we would walk out into the garden, soaking in the sharp winter sun. Lohri was celebrated while I was recuperating; I was given a place with the other members of the palace, the five queens, their children, the officers and their families. Thus, I was made to feel a part of a family. I was told that I could return to Lahore after Basant celebrations. My baba, Jivan Singh, had been informed of my extended stay in Kapurthala.

The first day after I returned to my senses, my host came to see me alone but thereafter he was invariably accompanied by a young girl whom he introduced as his niece, Harbans Kaur. Harbans was just twelve years old but she was sprightly and kept me entertained with stories that she concocted nineteen to the dozen. At first she fooled me into believing all the tall tales that she told me, but then I realised that she was simply letting her imagination run wild in order to keep me entertained while I was convalescing. At the Lohri celebrations I saw her singing and dancing merrily with her cousins. Her aunt and her mother eyed me with curiosity when they saw her chatting with me freely.

The next day, Maharaja Jagatjit took me by surprise when he asked me if I was willing to marry Harbans. I was unprepared for the question and had no answer. In his usual confident manner, he needed no answer and informed me that wedding nuptials would take place on Basant Panchami. Sardar Attar Singh and Baba Jivan Singh would be informed accordingly and they would attend the marriage. Thereafter, I would take the bride back home to Lahore.

So it was that on the auspicious occasion of Basant, when the sky was dotted with colourful kites and people were wearing yellow, when sweetened yellow rice was being served at family gatherings, Harbans and I took our holy vows and became man and wife. We returned to Lahore in the last few days of January 1913 and remained in baba's house while I completed my education. I did not – could not – go to England for further studies but I was in and out of Kapurthala and Amritsar where Harbans and I were always accorded a warm welcome.

I finished my education and worked for an insurance company, then I went to Burma where I worked for ten years as a forest contractor. Earning a regular livelihood was important for me because the privy purse that I was supposed to get from the royal house of Patiala could not be depended on. The Patiala family, like a huge spider, had spread its network wide and become large and unwieldy, with children and grandchildren, some legitimate, some not, some morganatic and others unacknowledged. The new maharaja had his hands full and his coffers had to cater to the needs of his own brood. I, being low in the priority list, was invariably overlooked. Finally I realised that I could no longer live in a state of uncertainty and that it was time to earn my own living instead of depending on a dole from the state. Harbans and I had a growing family, many mouths to feed, daughters to give away in marriage, and a regular income was essential.

Today, in 1952, I look back and realise that life has not always been easy but God has been kind. Living in free

India, I have the satisfaction that all my children and their families are doing well. I have not been able to go out of the country but my children and grandchildren are scattered all over the globe.

They do not know my story and I doubt if they ever will.

CODA

*L*ife is never fair! It does not deal you an impartial hand. If you are lucky you get by, but you are invariably caught in the meshes of a quirky fate and individual lives are sometimes sacrificed at the altar of politics. Higher powers intervene. By higher powers I am not referring to fate, destiny, God or any of those supernatural entities that one pontificates on. I have little faith in them. I am referring to the mortal, flesh and blood powers that exercise control on our terra firma. The king-makers, the control freaks, the power brokers, those who call the shots, those who decide the fates of other lesser mortals. Lesser mortals like me.

For the convenience of the powerful, some lives are snuffed out. Lives that could have been normal, healthy, happy, bubbling with vitality. Other lives are distorted or crippled, disguised or camouflaged, suffocated or maimed, or left to live somewhere in the margins where they pose no threat to the hierarchy. And still others are made to disappear like a bubble. They live but they do not live. They exist but there is no record of their lives. They are real, tangible lives but they may well be ghosts. Life passes them by. It sweeps through them and rushes on uncaring, unfeeling, unconcerned. These lives *are bulldozed because they are lives not within the scheme of things that matter and may easily be dispensed with.*

In this senseless deluge, love stories are left incomplete. Hearts are wrenched apart. Personal entities, individual lives get obliterated as history marches on. For the general good, for the progress of the nation, for world powers to coexist in peaceful conditions, certain lives, certain issues must be buried and some lives must be consigned to a living death. So they are assigned graves of anonymity.

This has been my case. Mine is the story of one who is alive – in the sense that I breathe, I am flesh and blood, I can feel, hear, speak, touch, and do whatever a living being is supposed to do. But in historical records I am dead. The powers that ruled then have consigned me to a living death. RRR is alive but he is dead. Kartar, who was dead, now lives on through me.

Thou shalt die but thou shalt also live. So it was decreed.

Do I go now to tell them I am still alive? But where is the proof? Where is the evidence? Who are my witnesses? The concerned people are no longer around. There is no one to vouch for me and I know I can never win my case so let me resign to my fate.

This is how a ghost must feel. This death in life.

The chill numbs my senses and I sink into nothingness.

When I swim back into consciousness I find that I am still at the ridge, propped up against the stone parapet. There is a crowd around me, poking and nudging, trying to get me on my feet. Here this evening, on this hilltop, looking down at the spot where four roads meet, I can see them milling around me but they do not see me looking at them. They act as though I am asleep or unconscious or even dead. They talk about me as though I were not present. I get up and walk away but they are still there, crowding around the *spot where I had sat musing. I leave them behind and walk away slowly towards Scandal Point.*

Through the gathering gloom, through the floating clouds, through the din of mixed voices carried by the breeze, I hear the loud clattering of hoofs approaching from a distance. Down the upper road that comes from the post office comes a dashing black steed with a turbaned rider. I see him larger than life. In the fading light he seems to radiate a strange glow. On his turban glints a huge ruby. Several strings of pearls adorn his neck. His spurs twinkle, his riding cloak is star-spangled. The smile on his face is triumphant as the horse halts suddenly and rears his forefeet high above the road.

From the other direction comes the sound of running feet and a girl in a blue dress and a dark riding cape materialises from nowhere. She reaches out to the horse-rider who, with one clean sweep, bends low and hauls her up on to the saddle.

They quickly ride away downhill, towards the west, with the high wind whistling in their ears, the road smoking behind them. The last rays of the setting sun glint on the ruby on the turban and light up a stray golden lock flying under the hooded cape.

They leave Scandal Point behind and move on.

They ride towards the last embers of a disappearing sunset.